SPECIAL MESSAGE TO READERS

This book is published by
THE ULVERSCROFT FOUNDATION
a registered charity in the U.K., No. 264873

The Foundation was established in 1974 to provide funds to help towards research, diagnosis and treatment of eye diseases. Below are a few examples of contributions made by THE ULVERSCROFT FOUNDATION:

A new Children's Assessment Unit
at Moorfield's Hospital, London.
•
Twin operating theatres at the
Western Ophthalmic Hospital, London.
•
The Frederick Thorpe Ulverscroft Chair of
Ophthalmology at the University of Leicester.
•
Eye Laser equipment to various eye hospitals.

If you would like to help further the work of the Foundation by making a donation or leaving a legacy, every contribution, no matter how small, is received with gratitude. Please write for details to:

**THE ULVERSCROFT FOUNDATION,
The Green, Bradgate Road, Anstey,
Leicester LE7 7FU. England
Telephone: (0533)364325**

I've travelled the world twice over,
Met the famous: saints and sinners,
Poets and artists, kings and queens,
Old stars and hopeful beginners,
I've been where no-one's been before,
Learned secrets from writers and cooks
All with one library ticket
To the wonderful world of books.

© JANICE JAMES.

BEFORE THE FACE OF THE SUN

This is an intimate look into the loves, hates, joys, and fears which touch all our lives. Set in the South Africa and Canada of the 1960's, the story has a timeless quality in its exploration of the good and evil in the human condition.

MOYRA F. LAWTON

BEFORE THE FACE OF THE SUN

Complete and Unabridged

ULVERSCROFT
Leicester

First published in Canada

First Large Print Edition
published June 1994

Copyright © 1992 by Moyra F. Lawton
All rights reserved

British Library CIP Data

Lawton, Moyra F.
 Before the face of the sun.—Large print ed.—
 Ulverscroft large print series: mystery
 I. Title
 813.54 [F]

ISBN 0-7089-3096-4

Published by
F. A. Thorpe (Publishing) Ltd.
Anstey, Leicestershire

Set by Words & Graphics Ltd.
Anstey, Leicestershire
Printed and bound in Great Britain by
T. J. Press (Padstow) Ltd., Padstow, Cornwall

This book is printed on acid-free paper

'You cannot separate the just from the unjust
and the good from the wicked;
For they stand together
before the face of the sun . . . '

The Prophet
Kahlil Gibran

1

THE merest spark of an idea first burned itself into Martin's mind soon after he and Flora were married in 1950. It was so shockingly evil that he had tried to blot it out, to pretend he had not thought of it, but he could not. Over the years it had remained in the recesses of his mind to worry him yet exhilarate. Now, suddenly, he wanted to act and knew he must be alone to think and to plan.

With a gesture of impatience he tucked the stethoscope into his black leather case and closed the clasp with a resounding snap, then glanced again at the digital wall clock where the second hand chased the numbers like an automated hare on a race track — 5:40, 5:41. It was late but he knew there was no way to hurry the old man dressing slowly in the adjoining examination room.

Above the low whir of the air conditioner a trapped fly buzzed angrily. Irritated,

Martin strode over and flung open the window, but the black insect clung persistently to the ledge.

"Idiot!" he muttered, swiping viciously, and it winged at last into the warm afternoon air.

Cape Town traffic roared on the Heerengracht below, then dulled to a quiet hum as Martin closed the window. He sat down at his desk, his long legs stretched out before him, and leaned back. He was tired of patients and their ailments, tired of his life and wished that someone could open a window for him. A muscle in his cheek twitched suddenly. As he pressed his fingertips against his jaw he looked thoughtful.

When the door of the examination room opened, he rose quickly and smiled mechanically at the patient shuffling toward him.

"Have this prescription made up before you leave for the farm, Meneer Retief," he said tearing a sheet from the pad in front of him, "and remember to take it just as I've told you." He patted his patient's thin shoulder reassuringly and guided him carefully toward the reception room door. He held it open.

"My secretary will give you an appointment. Three weeks from today, please, Miss Mears. Good-bye."

Then, with what he hoped would seem a friendly nod, he shut the door, cutting himself off too from the demands of his day, but it worried him that he had not been more charming to old Mr. Retief. He had been an Elder in his church for many years and was much respected. It would have been common decency to address him in his own language. The *Meneer* had been but a shallow token and insincere at that. Martin knew that he was prejudiced still against the Afrikaans-speaking people, still hostile and far too pro-English to be a good South African; a legacy from his English-born parents no doubt. Boer War hatreds were being carried down yet from generation to generation in the Republic; maybe even from him to his darling Beth, but that was something he did not have to worry about now. His daughter was well on the way to being a good Canadian in Alberta.

He sighed, tidied the papers on his

desk and gathered together some medical journals for later reading. He removed his white coat, folded it neatly and dropped it into the laundry bag, then slipped into his suit jacket and adjusted the shirt sleeves to the requisite inch below the jacket cuff. He fussed a moment with his Dior tie and smoothed his sparse sandy hair, trimmed to curl softly in the nape of his neck. Finally he surveyed his image in the mirror with a critical eye and began to feel more cheerful.

"Not bad for forty-one, really!" he murmured.

He picked up his hat and ran his sensitive fingers momentarily around the brim, then he stepped forward and whipped open the door to his secretary's office.

"Miss Mears!"

Small brown eyes looked up startled as she stumbled awkwardly to her feet.

"Yes, Doctor?"

"Why on earth do we work so hard? I'm absolutely exhausted and I'm sure you are too!"

He studied the small, plump figure before him: the crisp white uniform, the fastidiously manicured nails, the pale, crooked mouth, the thin greying hair. Poor old girl, he thought. I wonder if anyone has ever wanted to make love to her. It seemed unlikely. She was gentle, kind and dependable, but so uninteresting.

Suddenly conscious of her discomfort he looked away and headed slowly toward the exit.

"Maybe we need a holiday," he added softly. "Just leave everything as it is and get along home. We'll talk about this again."

"Yes, Doctor."

She smiled shyly and set down the notebook and pencil she had grabbed automatically at the sound of his voice.

As he closed the door he glanced at the black letters on the frosted glass of the upper half.

Martin Z. Nolan, F.R.C.S.
Urologist

Seeing his name and qualification in print (the fulfilment of a young dream) had always pleased him but now he wanted more — Pennington's Chair at the University of Cape Town when the old man retired. From a clinical practice in Urology to appointed Dean of the Faculty of Medicine would be to him a satisfying achievement and the prospect excited him. The powers that be must be made aware he was in the running. The rest would be a matter of strategy with his wife kept in the background where she could do no damage.

Slowly he moved along the corridor to the elevator, paused, then pressed the 'Down' button. A few seconds later the doors slid open and he stepped inside. At ground level he put on his hat, carefully tilted it to just the right angle and walked outside to the parking lot.

From the twelfth floor window of the reception room Molly Mears watched the tiny figure climb into his car, reverse from his allotted parking space and glide forward into the busy traffic. At the close of each working day she stood thus, unnoticed, and had done for many years. At first she had told herself it was to make sure that the doctor had gone for the night but later she was not so sure.

She spent most of her waking hours close to him or working for him and until this evening, he had never seemed to notice her, except as part of the décor. When those cold blue eyes had rested upon her she had felt naked and gauche. Her cheeks burned still from embarrassment.

Slowly she turned to collect her things. As Doctor had suggested, she too was exhausted and her canary would be waiting to come in from the balcony at home.

★ ★ ★

As Martin nosed his dark blue Mercedes up the steep slopes of Kloof Nek, flat-topped Table Mountain towered on his left while to the right Lion's Head and Signal Hill rose from the restless sea beneath. Tiny ships dotted at random the waters of Table Bay but Martin scarcely glanced at them. He drove over the Nek and turned into his favourite glen.

Tall trees nestled against the hillside and in their shade the earth was cool and the air filled with the tang of rotting leaves and moss. He breathed deeply, appreciatively, and looked down. The sea churned slowly against the rocks far below. To the left the peaks of the Twelve Apostles marched shoulder to shoulder, resplendent in their pine green cloaks. He did not care that he would be late for dinner, that the maid and houseboy would want to go off duty, or that Flora would have an extra drink or two while waiting for him. He had to decide, and soon, on a course of action.

His thoughts kept returning to the disastrous morning's meeting. He had quite expected to be nominated to the new committee and to be left out, in fact completely ignored, had been a severe blow to his pride, but now at least he would be prodded into action. He must cultivate a few people in the right places.

He wished now that he had accepted the invitation to the Medical Ball this evening. His students had seemed concerned when he told them he would not be going, and this had surprised him for he had made it abundantly clear that they were to be kept 'in their place' which meant, of course, two paces behind.

'Why don't you drop in for a while, sir?' one had said. 'Alone if your wife is not — er — well.'

Not well! Martin had almost snorted, unreasonably angry at the reference to his private life, but now he realized it might be a good idea to 'drop in' as the tactless but possibly well-meaning lad had suggested. He could make a start on Pennington. Turning on the charm had always been easy when he wished.

The golden sun dipped slowly beneath the ocean and the sky changed from the rosy hues of a summer's day to the colder, darker tones of the night. The mountains now stood grey and silent. Martin felt their strength and stability and was ready for home. He turned the ignition key, released the brake and headed for Camp's Bay.

★ ★ ★

Jackson, the houseboy, appeared as the car turned into the driveway and drew to a halt. Martin's face broke into a rare smile.

"Good evening, Jackson."

"Evening, *Baas*," the houseboy replied, leaning forward to open the car door with a flourish. Then he stood aside, black face shining and white teeth flashing a welcome. It was his duty to put the car away for the night and Martin knew it was the task he loved most. Leaving the keys dangling Martin climbed out and strode across the *stoep* into the house. As he hung his hat in the hall he heard the tinkle of glass.

"God!" he muttered. "I might have known!"

He moved quickly toward the lounge door and was just in time to see Flora gulp down the contents of her brandy glass. Her fair, freckled skin blushed a deep red when she saw him.

"Evening, my dear," Martin murmured, pecking her cheek coldly. Brandy and peppermint satiated his nostrils.

For Christ's sake, why must she chew peppermints, he thought savagely.

"I'm sorry I'm late," he said sharply. "Why don't you ring for dinner? I won't be a minute."

Flora reached for the bell as Martin

turned and left the room and when he returned she was seated in the low armchair staring into space.

"Dinner is served, Madam," came Jackson's voice from the dining room doorway.

Flora started to rise, then sank back. As Martin moved forward her head flopped despairingly on to her arms and she began to sob.

Martin glowered down in disgust on the untidy red hair, the low-cut, overbright tones of her blouse and the bony knees below the too-short skirt. His hands clenched into fists. He looked at Jackson still standing in the doorway and the gleam of contempt he saw in the black eyes was the proverbial last straw.

My wife! he thought. THIS IS MY WIFE! I could kill her! And he knew then that the little thought at the back of his mind would not go away. He had to try.

2

WITH Martin's harsh grip upon her arm Flora struggled to her feet. Half her mind screamed rebelliously at the indignity of being sent to bed like a disobedient child while the other half felt only relief that she would not have to spend the evening alone with him while he watched her over the edge of his book, pretending to read. This had always unnerved her but the last few weeks had been particularly difficult, her senses prickling with growing apprehension.

Sharp fingernails pressed into her flesh. "Martin! You're h-hurting me!" she protested, but he only held her more firmly, almost pushing her up the stairs and along to her room. As he helped her undress and prepare for bed she knew he was livid with rage and that she must not make the situation any worse. Through half closed eyes she watched warily as he closed the drapes and left the room, knowing he would go down the corridor to his bathroom. She heard the click of the medicine cabinet as he opened it, heard water splash into a glass and the cabinet bang shut. This meant pills and sleep. It was his way of getting rid of her, punishing her for misbehaviour, and tonight she had been ridiculously stupid. To have 'performed' in full view of the houseboy was just asking for trouble.

"Take these."

Martin's tired voice was low with tension. She felt a swift pang of pity but she stifled it. He deserved to suffer after all these years. He and Beth had cared little for her feelings when they had shut her out. She'd been hurt and angry at their love for each other, their closeness and self-sufficiency. Now it was Martin's turn. He'd been shaken and bewildered when his lovely daughter fell suddenly in love and even now, eighteen months since the wedding, Flora knew the hurt was still there. He would wander into Beth's room and sit brooding in her old easy chair, or stand looking out of the window as they had done together for so many years. Flora's whole being had cried out to go to him, to comfort him, but somehow she had managed to keep away. She could not face another rebuff. No! Not ever again!

She allowed herself to be propped up and obediently swallowed the pills he gave her. The water nauseated her. She lay back quietly and closed her eyes. She knew Martin was still standing beside her bed and agonizing fear caught at her. What did he do when he'd put her to sleep? Where did he go? She had no way of knowing. She concentrated on keeping utterly quiet and presently light footfalls receded across the carpet. She was alone.

Her thoughts flew back through the years. She must have been crazy to think of working her way half around the world so long ago, but there had seemed no other choice. When the call came that bleak afternoon at the insurance office, she had not realized the significance but had grabbed her raincoat and hat and dashed for the bus with but a scant word of apology to Mr. Wood, the supervisor. Her ailing father, alone during the day, had seemed weaker than usual the last two weeks, so this had appeared to be just one more call to her for help and comfort. On arrival home the neighbours were waiting for her at the front door, one crying silently into her handkerchief.

The shock had sent Flora staggering across the hall and into her father's room. Throwing herself across the bed she had sobbed 'Dad! Darling! Don't leave me! Please! You can't! I need you so much!' but it had been too late. Someone had taken her arm gently and led her away.

Later, somehow, she had managed to cope alone with the grim practical details. Jamie and Angus, her brothers, could be of no possible help from the 'outback' as they called it. When they emigrated to Australia at the end of the war they had made it abundantly clear that they must be unencumbered to work out their futures. She could see them now in her mind's eyes as clearly as that evening in the Spring of 1946, when they stood uneasily at the foot of their father's bed.

"We must go on ahead, Dad," Angus had said, his jaw thrust forward aggressively, as always, "to move around, find work, settle in, y'know! It's going to be mighty tough out there but there's no future here in England any more! You understand Dad?" He shifted his weight from one foot to the other, glanced down at his sister for a moment and then continued. "Flora will be here to look after you. She's a good girl and can cook just as well as old Ma used to and don't forget she'll soon be able to join the jolly old work force!"

He had laughed but Flora had begun to sob. She had seen herself growing old like her mother, with never enough of anything, her hands roughened and red from the everlasting drudgery that had shortened her life. Jamie, her darling Jamie, four years her elder, had taken her in his arms and whispered softly, 'Now, now! Kitten! You must be brave. It will not be long. I'll send for you as soon as I can. I promise!' But there had been no comfort in his words then and later no answer to her letters. She was not sure if he had heard about their father and the small sum that was waiting for him. She resolved to find him, not Angus.

When her share of the meagre inheritance was safely tucked away in her savings account she took the first step. She bought a steamship ticket to Cape Town, South Africa. The insurance company for which she had worked only briefly had been kind enough to arrange a temporary position there to enable her to save for the remainder of the voyage to Australia. That had been a great load off her shoulders.

A handful of friends waved farewell as she left by train for Southampton, where she was to embark, and as they disappeared from sight Flora's heart had given a great lurch. She would be among complete strangers on board and in Cape Town there would be no welcoming smile or friendly hug. She had an address in Sydney, Australia, but that was a long way away. Maybe she would never find her Jamie. He had never been keen on writing letters.

After two weeks on the ocean, Table Mountain had appeared in the distance. Spellbound she had watched from the ship's rail, scarcely changing her position, as the immaculate white cloth of cloud spread over the flat top and down the side like a real tablecloth. She would never forget that sight.

As she stepped uncertainly ashore, seagulls dipped and soared around her screeching a dubious welcome. She hurried along the dock, heading in the general direction of what seemed to be the city centre, her battered suitcase bumping awkwardly against her leg.

"Taxi? Taxi, Miss?"

The voice had startled her.

"Er — no thank you."

She was conscious of curious eyes following her and hurried on.

Soon the dockyards gave way to drab warehouses, squatting at intervals like shabby loafers, their barred windows heavy-lidded and dull, staring disinterestedly before them. Occasional potted geraniums provided the only splashes of colour, their brightness serving only to emphasize the greyness around them. A deep depression began to creep over her. She moved her suitcase from hand to hand, stepping now more warily as the setting sun dipped slowly behind the mountain. Fingers of fiery gold spread out across the sky as though touching the tops of the tall buildings with flame and gradually, one by one, like candles on a giant Christmas tree, the city lights flicked on around her. Panic caught at her throat like a vise. It would soon be dark. She struck out blindly across some railway tracks, hoping to cut off a section of winding road, but found her way barred by a heavy mesh fence.

"A cage!" she mouthed. "Just like a cage!"

She swung around to retrace her steps and almost froze in horror.

Three dark, leering faces cut off her retreat. In the half light they appeared in some devilish way detached from their limbs and bodies, then slowly their figures took shape. She watched, mesmerized. They spread out across the roadway and stood with hands in pockets, feet well apart. Their eyes roved over her body as though mentally undressing her. The lad in the middle spat contemptuously over his shoulder, then gave a hoot of laughter. His cap sat at a rakish angle on his bushy black hair. In a gesture of defiance he swung the peak to the back and took a step forward. His mouth opened in a lecherous grin. Flora's mind seemed to snap. She tried to scream but no sound came. Rigid with terror she managed to move her left foot an inch and then her right, and slowly — hardly daring to breathe — she began to edge along the wire fence.

"God help me!" she moaned. "Please God — anyone! Please help me!"

Dimly she heard the welcome sound of a car passing some fifty yards further on, and then another. She moved faster but ragged clothes and dirty bare feet moved faster too and closer as if playing a game with her — one for you and one for us, one for you and one for us!

Suddenly she found her voice. She screamed wildly and made a bolt for the road. She sensed rather than saw the figures spurt forward and the next instant they were upon her, jostling and pushing her and each other.

"Me carry bag for missy!"

"Why you all 'lone eh? Me go with you — find nice place to stay . . ."

Filthy hands tried to wrest the case from her. Faint from fear she held on frantically to all she possessed in the world and continued to scream as though her throat would burst.

A black hand closed over hers and the next moment her suitcase was wrenched from her grasp. She was thrown to the ground, her knees burning, her face stinging as it ripped across the coarse gravel. She lashed out in a frenzy but found herself pawing only air. Astonished, she realized her assailants were not at the moment interested in her but were fighting over her bag. It was pulled this way and that, then abruptly abandoned as they tore at each other.

Quickly she struggled to her feet. The next minute she was grabbed from behind and half carried, half dragged, bundled into the back seat of a car and her suitcase pushed in after her.

"Get going, Martin!"

"Well — shut the doors, you idiot!"

As the doors slammed, the car lurched forward on the rough and swung around on to the asphalt roadway.

Flora sat up and looked back through the rear window. The youths, finding their spoils whisked from under their noses, stood in the middle of the road angrily brandishing their fists.

"*Jou bleddie bastards!*" they shouted. "*Ons sal julle kry!*"

She did not understand but their meaning was clear. As she watched them fade into the darkness she started to shiver as if she had been placed on a vibrating belt. It was all she could do to straighten her clothing. Her stockings, torn and matted by drying blood, clung to her lacerated skin. She ached all over.

"Th . . . thank you!" she mumbled. "It was g . . . good of you to help me." Her jaw quivered still from shock. "Th . . . those terrible people . . . "

The swarthy young man who had pushed Flora into the car turned to glare at her.

"What on earth were you doing out there all alone? You're damned lucky we heard you yelling!"

Flora flushed.

"My . . . my ship had just docked. I was w . . . walking into town . . . "

"WALKING! My God! Well — you certainly weren't following the usual route. Why didn't you take a taxi?"

"I d . . . didn't think of it," she lied. How could she tell them she had wanted to save the fare — that she had very little money and it was still in British sterling?

"Well! You must be careful here, you know. These *skollies* are a real menace. By the way, that is a slang word for young hoodlums. They hang around waiting for drunk sailors or lonely dock workers and strip them of everything, if they get a chance, especially after dark. Women, of course, are fair game at any time. Surely someone warned you before you left the ship?"

"No. They didn't. I'd no idea. I thought it would be perfectly safe. You see I h . . . haven't much . . . " Her voice trembled away at the look of amazement on the man's face.

She dropped her eyes as he flashed her a quick smile, perhaps conscious that he had been too brusque.

"Well, anyway, you're safe now," he added. "We had been to a hospital near here — the Somerset. We were taking a short cut back to our flat. By the way, I'm Tom Meyer and this is Martin Nolan

— at your service!"

That had been Flora's introduction to Martin. Looking back over the years it seemed strange to her that she had scarcely noticed him at first. In the darkness he had seemed but a shadow beside Tom — kind, blundering Tom who had never stopped talking that night, as if the sound of his voice might take her mind off her problems. Tom had organized everything, the drive-in coffee stall, the visit to the hospital Emergency for her cuts to be dressed and finally the drive to the old Y.W.C.A. It was there in the harsh glare of the naked electric light bulb that she had looked closely at them both, but it was the tall, fair South African who had stirred her imagination. She had not been able to take her eyes from his softly tousled hair that gleamed gold in sharp contrast to blue eyes and deeply tanned skin. She had smiled shyly at him but he had not seemed to notice. A wave of coldness had seemed to emanate from him. She had felt a strong, almost overpowering urge to touch him, to warm him somehow, but it was Tom who had put a protecting arm around her shoulders and held her close.

"Don't worry, Flora," he had said, his kindly eyes meeting hers. "You've had a bad scare but don't worry. I'll look after you."

Later, as she lay in the narrow Y.W.C.A. bed with its cover faded by many washings, and watched the drab curtains stirring in the night breeze, Tom's words had recurred time and again to soothe her.

Now, so many years later, she lay in her own comfortable bedroom watching the breeze rippling the white nylon drapes like waves along the shore. The movement made her drowsy — the drug was taking effect. Her lids dropped, lifted and closed again.

"Oh, Tom!" she murmured. "If only you had looked after me."

Then she was asleep.

3

DISMISSING Flora from his mind, Martin seated himself at the dining room table and peered across at the dinner dishes that had been placed once more upon the heavy Stinkwood sideboard.

"And what is there tonight?" he asked Jackson, who was busy removing lids.

"*Bobotie* and rice with the usual trimmings, cauliflower and cream sauce, and a salad, with fruit salad for later, *Baas*."

Martin sighed. "Well! I hope Lizzie hasn't overdone the curry this time!" and they both laughed, for Lizzie, a Malay woman, was inclined to be a trifle heavy-handed with spices. Martin helped himself sparingly and began to eat mechanically while Jackson hovered in the background attending to his needs. The silence was broken only by the soft scrape of cutlery on crockery and the soft pad of white runners on the polished parquet flooring. When his coffee had been poured Martin sat back and looked at his houseboy.

"Are you still attending classes two nights a week, Jackson?"

"Yes, *Baas*."

"Doing well?"

"Oh! Yes, *Baas*."

"Good. Let me know when the next fees must be paid."

"Thank you, *Baas*."

"Oh! And Jackson . . . do you remember the discussion we had about the word *Baas*?"

"Yes, *Baas* — Doctor, Sir!"

"That's better! Remember I am not your master or 'Baas,' just your employer. I pay you to work for me but you are a free man and you have rights like any other working man. I believe Mr. Verwoerd made a big mistake when he introduced *apartheid* here, in our country. The world is watching now so this will have to change. You will see. So learn all you can now and be ready to play a peaceful part in helping your people."

"Yes, Doctor, sir!"

Martin smiled kindly at him. It

had been a most rewarding experience schooling this fellow and it was good to know that it was appreciated. Flora had always been afraid of him but Martin knew that he would never hurt anyone unless attacked. Their home was secure under his care.

All at once, Martin knew that he could not spend another evening in the stillness of that cold mausoleum of a house that he called home. He drained his coffee cup in one gulp and stood up, wiping his mouth hurriedly on a corner of his napkin before throwing it in a heap on the table.

"Jackson!" he said. "I'm sorry! I'll need the car again after all. Will you please bring it around in about half an hour. If anyone calls while I'm out I'll be at the Jamieson Hall at the University, but don't wait up. I'll arrange with the answering service to contact Dr. Mills."

"Yes, Doctor."

The black eyes looked curiously at him, but Martin did not explain. He hurried upstairs to shower, then hunted out his evening clothes, sprayed them hastily with air freshener in an amateurish effort to remove the odour of mothballs, and dressed quickly but with care. Anticipation almost paralysed his fingers when he reached the critical moment of attempting to knot his white bow tie, but finally this was accomplished. He stepped back to view himself in the mirror and was well pleased with what he saw.

★ ★ ★

The Ball was well under way by the time Martin reached the hall. As he mounted the stone steps the unfamiliar beat of a Samba pounded into the night. In the background the sound of shrill laughter and tinkling glass struck a jarring note. He halted uncertainly in the doorway, feeling suddenly out of things and alone. Whatever was he doing here? Everyone would be in parties. He'd look a fool going in now! She might not even be here! The whole idea was simply madness! He turned back and collided heavily with someone behind him.

"I'm so sorry!" he mumbled apologetically and then smiled in recognition. "Tom!"

"Why — Martin! You clumsy devil!" laughed Tom Meyer, limping exaggeratedly. "You might have injured me for life! Are you coming or going?"

"I was coming," answered Martin, "but I got an attack of cold feet! I'm going home again!"

"What nonsense!" exclaimed Tom cheerfully. "It's good to see you here, old chap. We're a man short now anyway. Come on! The party's just beginning to warm up."

Before he could protest, Martin found himself being drawn through the mob of dancers to a table of familiar faces near the band. His eyes swept searchingly around and then he saw her — the petite, dark figure across the table. He could have shouted 'She's here! Anthea's here!' but as always, he appeared outwardly cool, the complete gentleman, as he turned toward the elderly couple at the head of the table.

"Good evening, sir! Good evening, Mrs. Pennington," he said nodding formally and raising the old lady's fingertips to his lips in an old-world gesture.

He could see astonishment in the old man's eyes as he asked "You know everyone I expect, Martin?"

"Yes, thank you. I think so. Hello everyone!"

He raised a hand in greeting then turned again to the Dean's wife.

"It was good of you to come after all, Dr. Nolan," she said graciously, settling back in her chair like a well-preened duck. "We seldom see you at University parties. I'm glad you could get away. Please sit down." She indicated an empty chair beside her, then turned to her left. "You've met our new anaesthesiologist, Dr. Curtis?"

"Yes. How do you do," he answered and as his eyes caught Anthea's he could scarcely suppress a smile. Large eyes twinkled with amusement as if she knew why he had come. Martin nodded politely in her direction, remembering the moment, two weeks before in the Operating Theatre, when black-fringed green eyes had looked intently at him above her mask. He had read intelligence and interest in those eyes and something more that had been tantalizingly nebulous. His interest had been aroused but he had not been able to think of the future then. Now, tonight, things had changed. Without Flora — why! A whole new era of living lay ahead.

People were taking their partners for the next dance. Martin smiled at Anthea, his heart thumping disturbingly.

"Would you care to risk damaging your toes?" he asked. "I haven't danced for years!"

She smiled back, revealing little white teeth in a wide, generous mouth.

"I'd love to!"

A determined jaw was softened by a dimple in her cheek. A jewelled brooch nestling between her breasts glittered as she rose. Martin watched enthralled as she moved gracefully ahead of him on to the dance floor. She was more beautiful than he had remembered, but then ill-fitting operating theatre clothes had not been designed for glamour. Tonight her strapless white evening gown showed her tanned, slender figure to perfection and a sleek coiffure put the final touch to the picture she made of charm and elegance.

Martin held out his arms and as she moved close to him she looked steadily into his eyes. Her expression made him feel strangely embarrassed. Hurriedly he executed a few intricate steps. Anthea followed unhesitatingly. He chuckled, held her a shade closer and gave himself up to the unaccustomed joy of dancing. The years seemed to roll away.

When the music ceased she moved away from him.

"You misled me!" she commented with a mock bow. "I had to keep my wits about me then! It's your toes I'm worried about! Are they still intact?"

Martin laughed.

"They're just fine! They haven't skipped about so nimbly in years and I know they enjoyed it as much as I did."

He put his arm lightly around her to lead her back to their table. He longed to be alone with her to talk of serious things without the disturbing background of frivolity. His fingers tightened around her arm. He started to tell her, but they were already at their table and the moment was lost.

For some time he made a point of being charming to his colleagues' wives and to Mrs. Pennington in particular, while out of the corner of his eye he watched Anthea's every move and wondered about her.

"A great pity Dave was called away," said Tom as he replenished Anthea's glass, answering Martin's unspoken question. "I expect the staff in Casualty will be busy for several hours. Glad I wasn't on duty! It must have been a devil of a smash! All teenagers too I hear!"

"Yes. Simply ghastly isn't it?" he heard her say. "Poor parents!"

So that was it, Martin thought. The accident hardly registered as his spirits soared. Anthea's partner would not be back in time to take her home and, what was more important, Dave was happily married. He and his wife were expecting a baby any day now.

Martin quietly bided his time, danced a few duty dances and then, steering Anthea on to the floor for the last dance he said, "I hear Dave is still at the hospital. May I take you home?"

"Thank you. I'd like that," she answered.

"Oh, good!"

Martin twirled her dizzily around as the orchestra swung without a pause from one popular medley to another.

"I could have danced all night, I could have danced all night," sang the band leader.

Everyone joined in.

"I could have danced all night, I could have danced all night!"

The floor rocked as couples whirled gaily around together. Martin held Anthea close and knew he had wanted to do that all evening. He looked down at her and found her studying him with serious eyes. She smiled and Martin knew that he had passed her test.

4

OMINOUS clouds scurried across the night sky as the Mercedes purred along De Waal Drive toward the city. A few isolated raindrops danced on the windscreen then trickled gently down. Anthea and Martin watched in silence. Just a few moments before they had seemed so close. Now a yawning chasm of reserve separated them. Martin groped for the right words — ordinary everyday words — but they eluded him and the silence grew.

"I'm sorry!" he said at last, not knowing what else to say.

"Whatever for?"

"I've upset you."

"No! No!" she said with an embarrassed laugh. "I'm just a bit ashamed of myself, that's all. I don't usually give married men the advance-green signal quite as plainly as I did tonight. I'm sorry!"

"Well, I'm glad you did," he whispered and reached for her hand. He pressed her fingers softly and whistled. "You're ice cold! I should have warmed the car before we climbed in. Damn! I haven't even a coat to offer you."

"I'll soon warm up," she answered. "I have my wrap, but what about you?"

For a brief moment he felt the slim fingers tremble under his, then firmly, though gently, she withdrew her hand.

Martin smiled at her little show of primness and went on. "I never thought of bringing a coat — never thought of the weather — only that I might see you! Oh, dear! I had not meant to say that! Do you mind?"

She laughed. "Of course not, though I am a bit taken aback. The picture I had of the great Dr. Nolan is somewhat different."

"In what way?"

"Well — you do have the reputation of being a cold fish, you know!"

Martin put back his head and roared. "Is that so? And what else have you heard about me?"

Anthea hesitated momentarily then the words tumbled out like falling ninepins. "That you're a man of few words, dedicated to your work, a bit of a tyrant, egotistical, clever — even brilliant — a hater of women and — er — you keep your wife in a closet!"

She laughed brightly but Martin knew she was watching him in the dark — that this little thrust had been deliberate. Suddenly he was not amused. He did not want to hear any more — not now — and not from Anthea. A wave of misery and depression seemed to roll toward him, threatening to engulf him. He struggled against it, unable to speak, and the seconds grew to minutes. Then Anthea's hand touched his briefly, uncertainly.

"I've hurt you!" Her voice was almost a whisper.

"Not really," he said somewhat too brightly, finding words at last. "It was just — er — unexpected. I've always known my reputation, of course, but to realize that nothing is private in this rotten world, even one's hell, upsets me."

Anthea made no comment but Martin felt her hand slide softly along the sleeve of his jacket. Her cheek pressed against his shoulder. He could feel the rise and fall of her bosom as she breathed and he had a fierce longing to place his hand on her breast, to feel the velvet of her skin, to put his lips against hers.

Suddenly there was a low rumble above them, followed by a deafening crash of thunder. They both jumped and Anthea sat up.

"My gods are telling me to beware of you!"

She laughed, smoothing her hair into place.

Martin made an effort to smile but his eyes were stern as he looked ahead. A few words had ruined his evening and now the weather!

Sheets of dense rain, whipped by the wind, poured down on them as though trying to sweep them off the road. He changed down to a crawl but the action was automatic. Through the windscreen he saw only the image of Flora as she had looked earlier, a drop of brandy about to fall from her parted lips.

The next moment, without warning, a dark shape loomed up before them.

"What on earth?" yelled Martin and

swung the wheel hard over as he jammed his foot down on the brake. The car skidded past a stationary camper, across the road and partly down the opposite embankment, jerking to an abrupt stop inches from the edge.

Both were shocked into silence but presently Martin opened the window slowly, carefully, and leaned out. Rain pelted down upon his bare head but he was unaware of it. He could only stare aghast at the lights far below twinkling like distant glow-worms dropped from the black night.

"My God! We're right on the edge!"

"I know. Don't move. I think this front wheel is almost over." Her voice was soft.

The flesh on Martin's back seemed to crawl with a thousand ants. Cautiously he withdrew his head and felt for the gearshift.

"We'll drop like a rock if it goes," he murmured.

"Don't think about it! I'll lean back as far as possible, but be careful!"

"Can you climb to the back to open the rear door?"

40

"No. The movement might push the front wheel over."

Martin's lips began to quiver. Jesus! Don't let me break down! Not now! He took a deep breath, grasped the gear lever firmly yet gently and put the car into reverse. Stealthily he released the brake. The wheels spun noisily and ineffectually over the loose earth a few moments, then they held and inch by inch the Mercedes crept up to the narrow shoulder and on to the road.

He had made it, but Martin's knees were like jelly quivering in a bowl.

"You were magnificent!" was all that Anthea said, but she moved close and rested her head on his shoulder.

Rare emotion tore at him. He clenched his jaw together until they ached, grateful that Anthea did not chatter, and presently they were edging into the intermittent stream of slow-moving traffic. Martin concentrated on steering the car safely down the mountain side toward the harbour and shore. The foghorn moaned at intervals and the lighthouse beam lit the sky dimly as it revolved in the deluge. Rain was still falling as he drew the car up under the entrance canopy of her apartment building and climbed shakily out, but he now had control of himself. He was conscious of Anthea's eyes following him as he walked around to her side and held the door open for her and he realized that she didn't want to leave him any more than he wanted to leave her. Their eyes met.

"You can't possibly go on," she said, stepping out. "Come inside for a drink and wait until the storm is over."

"May I? Thank you," he said. "The drive over the Kloof won't be much fun if there's a repetition of that cloudburst."

His words sounded stilted but Martin knew she understood that what he really wanted was to be alone with her in the quiet of her flat.

He parked a short distance on and ran quickly back. Rain had matted his thin hair and ran in rivulets down his neck and inside his collar. He saw Anthea waiting for him in the lobby and hastily brushed himself down with his handkerchief. Together they climbed the flight of stairs and a picture flashed disturbingly across Martin's mind, a picture of Flora held firmly in his grasp as they mounted the stairs at home before dinner. He stumbled.

Anthea turned questioningly toward him and, as if she knew what was in his mind, she held out a helping hand.

"This has been quite an evening for you, hasn't it?" she asked softly. "I think you can do with that drink!"

As she turned the key in the lock and opened the door, it occurred to Martin that it would always be difficult to keep anything from Anthea and this might prove extremely awkward, if not calamitous.

★ ★ ★

Inside, Anthea placed the whiskey decanter, soda siphon and a couple of glasses on a small table, then busied herself making coffee in the kitchenette.

"Please make yourself comfortable," she called "and pour the drinks will you? Very little whiskey for me but lots of soda, please."

Martin poured the drinks, then looked around him with interest. Anthea's room was markedly different from Flora's gaudy furnishings and fussy knick-knacks. Here the effect was elegant yet simple, the room resembling more a study than a lounge. He chose a low leather chair beside the empty fireplace and sat down rubbing his cold hands together. He felt chilled and wished a fire had been burning in the grate. Contemporary paintings and ornaments blended with Dutch antiques, lending an air of quiet restfulness. Rows of books covered one wall. Martin scanned the titles.

"You have a fine collection of books, Anthea," he said as she entered with the tray. He rose to take it from her and as he used her given name for the first time he caught her glance.

"You don't mind?"

"Of course not."

She looked across at him and smiled.

"You can see that books fascinate me. They always have though I don't ever seem to have enough time now to satisfy my appetite. How do you like your coffee? Black?"

"Yes, please. No sugar."

They sipped their drinks and coffee

quietly, companionably, chatting of their work at the hospital and of the Annual Ball. Martin made no move to go. He wanted to know all about this fascinating creature, what she thought, how she lived. He'd not scratched the surface veneer of acquaintanceship as yet.

"I've been wondering," he said. "How did you come to take up anaesthesiology?"

"I drifted into it really. Rather reluctantly too!" she added, her voice suddenly tense. "I'd always wanted to be a surgeon. I had great dreams. When I qualified I went into general practice for a time — a group practice — but there were too many frustrations. Do you know what I found the biggest handicap?"

"No. What?"

"Being a woman!"

"A handicap!" Martin chuckled.

"No, don't laugh!" she said. "I feel very strongly about this. The work didn't satisfy me and I knew it never would. There were too many coughs and colds and sore tummies, nothing really challenging. All the interesting work went to the men or had to be referred to specialists."

She broke off and rose from her low chair. "Would you like another drink?"

"No, thank you. But may I have some more coffee?"

"Of course."

When she was again seated she went on.

"I wanted to be on my own, to be solely responsible for what I did. I toyed with the idea of gynaecology at first, but as you know it is difficult to divorce it entirely from obstetrics. I'd never fancied obstetrics — or pediatrics for that matter! Too much night work in the one and the other too distressing seeing small children ill and helpless day after day. It was the operating theatre that intrigued me, but I had to be realistic about it. Not much general surgery would be sent my way!"

She curled up more comfortably in her chair and looked at him.

"Incidentally, have you noticed what a rare species the female general surgeon is in our society?"

Martin nodded. "Yes, though I had always assumed you ladies have not the stomach for the gory business of butchering!"

He smiled at her and Anthea laughed.

"At least you didn't say we are not capable!"

Martin chortled. He was enjoying himself again.

Anthea continued.

"Anyway, I settled for a different aspect of the operating theatre. I don't think I am sorry but it is a bit early to be sure. I gave up a great deal along the way but what is more important I've allowed my life's stream to be diverted. It could prove to be the wrong decision."

Martin nodded understandingly.

"So many of us drift into unplanned channels, don't we? My life isn't exactly as I'd planned it either. Sometimes things turn out well, sometimes we are not so lucky. One wrong turn can ruin one's life."

Anthea glanced quickly in his direction.

"I'm sorry!" she said softly. "I know what you are trying to tell me, but your life isn't ruined from what I can see. You have more than most, far more! And surely your difficulties are capable of some solution, or do you enjoy sitting back feeling sorry for yourself?"

Martin tapped thoughtfully on the arm of his chair.

"Maybe I do," he answered. "I probably could make life a lot easier for myself if I tried, but things seem so hopeless sometimes."

"I have a good idea how things are at home for you," Anthea continued. "People talk, you know. You must feel desperate at times."

Martin looked quickly at her but she had risen and was busy placing the coffee cups on the tray.

"It's incredible that we met only two weeks ago," he said. "You seem to know me so well. And I feel, somehow, that I've known you always."

She smiled. "So you don't remember me!"

"Remember you?"

"I've known you for years."

"You have?"

"Yes, though not socially. I used to attend your lectures, but that's quite a while ago. By now I know a good deal about you, and your life and work too."

"Well — I'll be damned!" he exclaimed. "I thought you'd just come from England."

"Yes, but I went over to study and write my post-graduate examination."

"Oh, I see."

"All evening I was wondering if you'd remember me. I looked for that little spark of recognition when we first danced together, but I was disappointed. It was silly of me, of course. I've changed a lot in recent years."

"I'm sorry," Martin said. "But maybe I did remember subconsciously. When I saw you in the operating theatre two weeks ago I knew there was something very special about you. I almost felt as if I'd known you in a previous life! Have you ever had that feeling? I had to keep a firm grip on myself to keep sane!" and he laughed.

Anthea smiled. She drew up a stool near Martin's chair and sat looking up at him, then she turned away, clasping her hands around her knees.

"I often thought about you when I was a student," she said softly. "You were good-looking, successful, highly regarded. You seemed to have everything, yet you lacked animation, almost as if you were waiting for life to be breathed into you.

I couldn't understand it. It didn't seem natural, then, of course, I heard of your difficulties with your wife. Are you still unhappy?"

"Yes. I try not to think about it," he answered.

"But isn't that running away? Can't you face up to the problem squarely and see if it can be changed?"

Martin looked down at the silky head so near to his own.

"It's odd that you should mention this now," he said. "Only tonight I decided to do just that!" Anthea turned her head to look into his eyes as though trying to read them.

"What happened between you?" she asked. "Would you like to tell me about it?"

Martin frowned. How could he possibly tell Anthea. Tell anyone!

"That is something I never talk about," he said firmly. "But then, there is nothing to tell really. It's the usual story. We should never have married! It's as simple as that. We were far too young for a start. As the years passed we drifted apart — it was inevitable. We had nothing in common. Our daughter gave me the only real happiness I knew, but she is married now. She lives in Canada. There was always my work but, now, that doesn't seem enough. I feel trapped! Cheated!"

He stopped. The grandfather clock in the hall ticked loudly in the silence.

"I know how you must feel," Anthea said softly, resting her hand gently on his arm, "but is it too late?"

They looked searchingly at each other. Then Martin spoke quietly.

"I'd almost forgotten there was such a thing as happiness until tonight!"

"Yes. You were happy, weren't you?"

Martin put out his hand and touched her soft hair.

"That just shows what you can do for me," he said. "I feel alive again."

His fingers caressed her cheek. Then he put his hand under her chin and tilted up her face so that he could look at her.

"You are very beautiful," he said. "It wouldn't take much for me to fall in love with you, but you know that. I think that you could love me a little too, if you don't fight it."

Anthea smiled up at him.

"I don't know," she said. "For years I had a clear picture of my Prince Charming but he was a god, remote, inaccessible. I always knew that he was not for me and I accepted this, but he spoiled other men for me. I kept telling myself that I was too busy. I made myself busy!"

She turned away and commenced poking at the empty grate with the toe of her shoe.

"But what do I do now if I find my god is no longer inaccessible? The feelings I had — were they born of admiration, a need to be cherished, or were they the beginning of love? I don't know. I don't know what love is. Perhaps it will be as well if I never know! I've never wanted any hole-in-the-corner affair and what else could there be for us?"

She swung around, took his hands in hers and looked at them, then rested them a moment against her cheek.

"You must go now," she continued. "There seems to be a lull in the storm. Try to get home before the next downpour if you can."

She rose, pulling him up with her, and the next moment they were in each other's arms. The softness of her, the delicate fragrance of her hair, made his senses leap.

"Oh, why didn't I meet you before?" he murmured, his lips against her hair. "What are we going to do?"

For an age they stood, while all the suppressed emotions of the last years seemed to flood Martins' being.

"I knew this would happen when we met tonight," Anthea said. "I wanted it to happen! I'm sorry! It's my fault entirely. I should not have encouraged you. Now we'll have to work this out. It's another unplanned channel, isn't it?"

She drew away and walked briskly into the hall. Reluctantly Martin followed, and as Anthea placed her hand on the knob of the front door he put his arms around her to draw her back, but she swung to face him with her arms outstretched and smiled up at him.

"No, not now, Martin," she said firmly. "Good night."

"Good night, Anthea."

He hesitated a moment, then he leaned

forward, kissed her lightly on the top of her head and walked into the corridor. As he left the building the cold seemed to wrap itself around him and he shivered. By the time he reached Camp's Bay he realized he had caught a severe chill.

Inside the silent house he poured himself another whiskey. He swallowed a couple of tablets, sat down in his favourite chair and sipped his drink slowly. Gradually the shivering lessened, but he felt far from well. Dragging one foot after the other he climbed the stairs to his room, undressed and crept into bed. He did not look in to see if his wife was all right. He had forgotten all about her.

5

MARTIN mopped at the perspiration that kept beading on his forehead and trickling down the back of his neck. He had scarcely slept all night, plagued by a troubled mind, a rising fever, and aching chest.

When Jackson quietly slid the early morning tray on to the bedside table the aroma of coffee wafted his way. Warily Martin opened one eye and looked up.

"Just iced water, please. I don't feel at all well."

"I can see, Doctor. Oh, my!" and he bent solicitously forward to straighten the bedcovers. "Shall I telephone Miss Mears?"

Martin nodded. "Tell her to cancel all my engagements for a few days at least. I'll call her later."

"Yes, Doctor. I'll see to that right away," and with a worried frown he padded quickly from the room.

Martin plumped up his pillow and lay

back trying to find a cool spot to rest his flaming cheek. His mind was awhirl with pictures of people long forgotten, popping in and out of his consciousness, and now suddenly there was his mother as he had last seen her, sitting beside him, a cool damp handkerchief in her hand for mopping her brow as of old. She had seemed so real he almost smelled the eau de Cologne she had used. She would have been over sixty now if she had lived, yet he always thought of her as young. She had not wanted to go for the ride in the fast, flashy sports car his father had bought for himself, but as always she had bent to his will. When the young fisherman found the wreck they must have been dead for some hours, the front half of the car submerged in six feet of water below a sharp curve on the scenic drive to Oudekraal. The report had read, 'Death by drowning.' That had happened so long ago, yet she had seemed to be right here with him just a moment before. A sob rose in his throat. He turned his face to the wall and tried to sleep.

It was close to lunchtime before

Martin was awakened by the sound of a car driving up to the house. Low voices sounded in the hall, then heavy footsteps trod the stairway to Martin's room. He struggled to sit up and the next moment Tom Meyer's smiling face appeared behind Jackson's anxious one in the doorway.

"What's all this about feeling ill?" asked Tom in his usual breezy manner as he gestured to the houseboy to leave them. "Too old for fun with the girls, eh?" and he guffawed loudly.

Martin managed a feeble smile. "Not at all! It's just my chest, Tom."

"What a disappointment! Anyway — let's have a look at you."

Deft fingers tapped and the stethoscope was moved about methodically. Then Tom straightened up and replaced the bed covers.

"Humph!" he said, examining the aspirin bottle on the bedside table. "You are going to need more than those, that's for sure!"

He slipped a thermometer between Martin's lips and continued.

"And now that you can't answer back

I've got something to say!"

He sat down on the edge of the bed and looked at Martin, but Martin's eyes were closed.

"We've known each other a long time now and though we aren't as close as we once were, I'm still fond of you, too fond to sit back and watch you make a complete ass of yourself!"

He was silent a moment but Martin did not answer. His eyes remained shut. Tom shifted his position slightly and then continued.

"I never really understood about you and Flora — but we won't go into that now. You've made a damned hash of your marriage and if you don't watch out you'll foul it up even more."

Martin made a move to take the thermometer out of his mouth, but Tom was too quick for him.

"No, old chap! I've got you listening quietly for once, so let me finish."

He leaned back and cradled one knee in his hands. Then he continued.

"I'm a pretty good judge, you know! Maybe it's my old bachelor eye for a skirt, eh? Anyway, I spotted which way the wind was blowing with you and Anthea last night. Now, I don't blame you. Something like this was bound to happen, but I want to warn you. If you start an affair with that girl you'll be sorry. Have an affair by all means! In fact I think it is just what you need, but find someone out of town and keep her out of sight. It may be an underhanded thing to do, but it's the only way for a doctor. If you value your position, take a trip — go overseas, anywhere — but get away for a while. Why don't you visit Beth? Isn't she having a baby soon? A change would do you a world of good, and Flora too! She's going downhill more rapidly now that Beth has gone. You don't care, obviously, but I don't like to see it. She was an attractive girl once and I was very fond of her, but you knew that didn't you?"

Martin's head moved impatiently on the pillow but he remained silent.

Tom continued.

"Why don't you try to make a go of it again? It would not take much effort on your part to help Flora over her few hurdles. Half her trouble is that life holds nothing for her."

He leaned forward, removed the thermometer from Martin's mouth and held it to the light from the window.

"My God!" he spluttered. "If this gets any higher you'll be in Hades! You must take care, old man! Lie low for a while, in more ways than one!"

He chortled and Martin's eyes flickered open. For a second they gazed at each other without speaking, then Tom put out a hand and touched his friend gently on the shoulder.

"I'm sorry," he said. "I'm a swine to kick a chap when he's down! I didn't mean to, you know. I only want to help. It does worry me to see you always so unhappy, but things must surely improve. Why — Flora's liver may even pack up and you and Anthea will be able to get married! Who knows?"

Seeing Martin's startled eyes shift to the doorway, Tom swung round. His mouth fell open. Flora stood in the doorway, her hair an untidy heap upon her shoulders, one hand clutching her gown to her breast and the other resting for support on the door frame. She looked steadily at Tom as he rose slowly to his feet, then she turned and walked quietly away. A few moments later they heard her door close.

"Oh! Damnation!" spluttered Tom. "My big mouth again! I had no idea she was home! When Miss Mears phoned me, and after last night, I thought Flora must be away. She heard me! I'm so sorry!"

Martin waved his hand feebly.

"Don't worry, Tom. A few swigs of brandy and she'll think she dreamed the whole thing! It was good of you to come. I appreciate it. I'd no idea my secretary had phoned you but I'm glad she did. I'll think about what you said. Maybe a long holiday is what we need right now."

Tom, still shaking his head with embarrassment, delved into his big brown bag. He removed a couple of containers and carefully counted out some pills.

"You will have to have that chest X-rayed, of course, and I'd feel happier if you had an ECG too. You seem to have been pushing yourself a bit hard lately, I don't know why. In the meantime, we can try you on these."

He scrawled on a label and placed a pill box on the table. "And shall I leave some sleeping pills?"

Martin nodded. "Please. I don't keep drugs around the house now, as you can understand, and I could do with a good sleep."

Tom looked as if he were about to say something, but he merely counted out a few more pills, wrote on a label and placed another box on the bedside table.

"Now I must get along," he said, clicking his bag shut. "Look after yourself, old boy. If you need me, ask Jackson to telephone. I'll be along in the morning. Now, I'll just wash first, if I may."

He swung around and walked into Martin's bathroom. As he stood washing his hands he glanced above to the glass-fronted medicine cabinet. Among others stood two small bottles clearly labelled in large letters. He looked hard at them. They were both full.

"That's interesting!" he muttered, wiping his hands on a guest towel, and a few minutes later he had gone.

* * *

Several days passed before Martin felt well enough to get up for breakfast. He had kept in touch with his office and all emergencies had been taken care of by the inimitable Miss Mears. He was enjoying the leisure. Tom was right. Why not take a holiday? It had been years since he'd had a good break and a slow voyage might provide just the opportunity he needed.

He was eating his toast and marmalade when Flora entered the room and sat down opposite him at the table. Martin almost choked with astonishment.

"Just dry toast and black coffee, please," she said as Jackson appeared.

Martin had not seen her since the unfortunate morning when Tom had first come to visit him and he hardly recognized her. Her eyes were still swollen and her face blotchy but she was neatly dressed and her hair swept back smoothly, tied with an attractive green silk scarf. It was obvious she was completely sober and this set Martin wondering. Was it the shock of Tom's words that had sobered her, or did she always look better in the mornings? He realized that he did not know.

While Jackson made the toast and poured out the coffee, Flora was silent, but when he left the room she said, "I wanted to talk to you."

She cut her toast into tiny pieces and began crumbling them between her shaking fingers. Martin had already formulated answers to the unspoken questions that he sensed were coming, but he waited for her to go on.

"Who is Anthea? How long has this been going on?" she asked at last. Her voice was low, restrained.

Martin deliberately drained his coffee cup, wiped his mouth and folded the table napkin before he answered,

"Nothing has been 'going on'," he said irritably. "That was just one of Tom's bad jokes. The girl is a doctor at Grooet Schuur. She arrived a couple of weeks ago. We all kid each other about her. She's a fine girl. Tom's teasing very often goes a bit too far, as you know. Now, please forget the whole thing, or at least don't refer to it again!"

Flora stared into space as if weighing his words, then she picked up her coffee cup, held it in both hands to keep it steady, and commenced to sip slowly. Martin watched her in silence. He could almost see her small mind ticking over. He'd been such a fool to get involved with her.

Flora lowered her cup carefully and looked closely at him.

"And you really think I shall believe that?" she asked.

"You may believe whatever you wish," he snapped. "I don't have to explain my actions to you!"

Flora sighed and picked up her cup again.

"I like to know what you are up to," she said. "To keep tabs, as it were! I've always known of your amorous adventures in the past. There are ways of knowing — just little things — but enough. The scent of a strange perfume still lingering on your clothes, your flushed face or perhaps even a guilty look you could not hide. Yes. I've known. It used to hurt terribly! I didn't understand. I was here and I loved you. I thought that might give me an edge over the others, but my love meant just nothing to you, nothing at all! You have always wanted to hurt me. You still do."

Martin lifted the coffee spoon off his saucer and tapped it against his cup. He knew he would have to watch his temper. Snapping at her was no way to convince his wife that they should all play the little game of Happy Family when they got to Canada. He leaned back in his chair and smiled suddenly.

"You always were a bit of a fool," he said, but his tone was jocular. Flora looked at him over the edge of her coffee cup and Martin saw a wary look come into her eyes. It was almost as if they said, 'and what is he up to this time?'

He grinned across the table.

"I don't think I'll tell you of the surprise I'm planning. I'll go alone and have a glorious time."

"What do you mean?"

Martin laughed. "It was Tom's idea. He thought we should take a trip. How would you like to visit Beth after the baby is born?"

Flora's cup clattered on to the saucer.

"You mean it? You really mean it? The two of us?"

"Certainly. There is a medical congress I'd like to attend in London in May. We can go to Canada first to be with Beth and Arthur and get acquainted with the little one. I haven't worked out any details of course, but I'll ask Miss Mears to see to it when I return to my office."

Martin could see the flush of excitement that had flooded Flora's face and neck, but he was far from happy. He wished he had not mentioned the trip until he'd had time to perfect his plans. He dreaded the thought of coping with Flora's probable bad sessions, but even that could be worked out, he felt sure. He could send her on ahead, but it must look as if it were Flora's own idea.

"If I have too much to clear up here we could perhaps fly over and come back by ship," he said.

"Oh, no! Please Martin!" entreated Flora. "You know how terrified I am of flying and these days, with all the hi-jacking . . ."

Martin could scarcely suppress the

smile that broke out.

"Very well then," he said. "We'll see about someone to accompany you by ship. I'll fly over later."

"Yes. I'd like that."

Martin was delighted. Her reaction was exactly as he had anticipated. He would be able to spend a few weeks alone with Anthea and Flora would never know. He felt that he held the fate of mankind in his hands, that he could manipulate lives to order like puppets on a string. He felt expansive and generous.

"You will probably need some extra clothes," he said. "Why don't you go into town this morning? You seem well enough. Jackson can drive you."

Flora pushed back her chair and rose, leaving her coffee unfinished.

"Yes, thank you," she said. "I think I will."

She smiled fleetingly, then hurried from the room, her mules clicking faintly across the hall and up the stairs.

Martin was still smiling to himself as he walked slowly into his study. He felt that he had handled the situation most adroitly. Flora now had the voyage to look forward to instead of worrying about Anthea. The shopping had been a brilliant idea too. She would be busy for weeks trying on all the newest clothes in town. He reached for his cheque book. Keeping Flora happily unsuspecting would be well worth the price. He filled in a cheque and signed his name with his usual illegible flourish.

6

ON Martin's return to his office his secretary plunged immediately into the intricacies of holiday planning, and a few days later Molly Mears, the picture of smug efficiency, leaned across Martin's desk and pointed with her pencil to the neat typewritten itinerary she had arranged with the travel bureau.

"This schedule should work out well, Doctor," she said. "As you will see, your wife can sail on the 12th of March for Halifax, then continue by train to Edmonton. You can fly over to Canada early in May and spend about three weeks with your family before flying to London for the medical congress while your wife again travels by train and ship. You will be able to meet her when she lands in Southampton and together board your ship for home. I've arranged for Gladys McGill to travel with Mrs. Nolan, as you suggested."

She stopped and Martin realized he had completely lost the gist of what she had been saying. He had been engrossed in calculating. Quickly his eyes sped across the sheet. Yes. He had it now.

"Thank you, Miss Mears," he said. "That sounds perfect, but what ship is this you have arranged for the return voyage?"

"She is the *S.S. Glenconnor*," Doctor. She is one of the older ships of the line but her sailing date is just right. She is due to arrive in Table Bay Docks on the 15th of June, which means you will be away for about six weeks, as you wished."

She straightened up and smiled, reminding him of a rather overweight little dog waiting anxiously for a word of praise from her master before wagging her tail with joy. Martin, amused at her obvious satisfaction, smiled back.

"You've done an excellent job, Miss Mears," he said looking straight at her. "I couldn't have done better myself!"

He watched the colour quickly sweep across her face and down her neck. Poor simple little soul, he thought. She had not realized he had meant it more as a joke than a compliment.

Still smiling he inclined his head to signify that the interview was over, and when she had gone he leaned over and picked up the desk calendar. Seven precious weeks to devote to Anthea and then to the business of Flora. He flipped the pages over, one by one, stopped at the fourteenth, then turned back a page. The 13th of June. Two nights before his arrival in Cape Town. It should be as good as any. Flora had always been ridiculously superstitious about the number thirteen. He considered it lucky. With a firm stroke he encircled the figure in a black felt pen, then sat back, stretching his long legs out before him in his usual relaxed manner when alone. Not long to wait now. No, not long at all, he thought, but he was wrong.

With his irrevocable course set, the days until Flora's departure seemed like a rosary stretched out on a line to eternity. He became restless and irritable, snapping at nurses and patients alike. When at last the great day arrived, he felt near to the breaking point, his nerves taut from anxiety that for some trifling reason Flora would be unable to sail as planned. Again and again he checked all important items: tickets, passport, vaccination certificate, traveller's cheques, Canadian dollars, rands, and change. Now, ill at ease, he watched last minute preparations.

Lizzie had been summoned from the kitchen to lend her ample weight. She was now seated giggling upon the largest suitcase endeavouring to weigh it down sufficiently for Jackson to fasten the clasps. As she bounced Jackson heaved, then they dissolved into paroxysms of laughter while Flora flitted helplessly about picking up bits and pieces of clothing and putting them down again.

From time to time Martin glanced anxiously at his watch, exasperation mounting. If they did not hurry Flora would be late. She was due on board at least one hour before sailing time and there was still the drive to the docks and the luggage for the hold to check in — both time consuming. He began to pace the floor. She had had nothing to do for weeks but get ready. Women like Flora were impossible! They literally muddled through their lives. He had no patience with them. Inefficiency was inexcusable! He muttered under his breath and prayed he would not explode in anger before the servants. But at last the catches were secured, the luggage labelled and placed in the car and they all trooped downstairs.

As Flora reached the car she turned suddenly to look back at the house. Lizzie, so happy only moments before, now stood on the *stoep* with tears streaming down her cheeks. Then, mopping her eyes with the corner of her apron, she waddled awkwardly down the steps and stopped in front of Flora.

"Be careful, Madam," she whispered, grasping Flora's hand between her two brown ones, "very careful! The sea is bad luck! I'm afraid for you!"

Flora smiled gently. "Everything will be all right, Lizzie. I'll be safe I'm sure," and bent forward to embrace the kind-hearted woman who had been more friend than servant for some ten years. Then she climbed into the car and waved until the curve in the driveway hid Lizzie from view.

"And what was all that about?" asked Martin in a frosty tone.

"Oh! Lizzie was just anxious about the sea. She says it is bad luck and that I must be careful."

"Well I do wish you would remember there is such a thing as *apartheid* in this country. It is not wise to embrace in public, and your maid at that!" He had lowered his voice but felt sure that Jackson had heard every word though he gave no sign as he sat behind the wheel.

Flora turned her head to look straight at her husband.

"I can't believe you said that! You of all people! First of all, this is hardly a public place. It is where I live! Secondly, caring, compassion, even love are expressions from the heart — not dictated by status or colour of the skin!" She turned away and stared out of the window leaving Martin speechless with anger. He saw Jackson looking at him in the driver's mirror and decided that further speech would be useless at present. He turned to look out of the window on his side and they drove the few miles to the docks in silence, turned in through the dock gates and over to the parking lot.

The *S.S. Fengu Girl* was a small vessel with accommodation for a dozen passengers. Cranes fore and aft were still busy loading freight as Martin and Flora climbed on board and followed the baggage steward to No. 5. The cabin was fairly large and looked comfortable. A washroom, with shower and toilet, led off to the right.

"Who is in charge of this cabin?" asked Martin as the steward deposited the suitcases Flora would need for the voyage and stood hopefully waiting.

"I am, sir."

"I'd be grateful if you would keep an eye on my wife and her companion and make sure they have all they need," he said and held out his hand.

As the steward felt the wad of notes Martin saw his eyes lighten.

"I'll sure take good care of them, sir," he said. "Don't worry!" Then with a big smile and a half salute he was gone.

Martin glanced into the empty cabin next to Flora's.

"Miss McGill should have been here

by now," he remarked, eyes once again on his wristwatch. "It's strange. There is no sign of luggage. She's certainly cutting it very fine! I don't like this — don't like it at all."

He wandered down the short corridor to the main gangway, studying figures and faces, but there was no sign of Gladys McGill.

"Dr. Nolan?"

Martin swung around. It was the steward.

"This message has just arrived, sir."

He held out a folded sheet of paper and even before Martin read it he knew what it contained. As he strode back to the cabin the muscles in his jaw twitched with anger.

"What is it?" Flora asked, her voice tremulous.

Martin sat down on the edge of the berth and thrust the paper into Flora's hand.

"She won't be coming!" he barked.

"Who? Miss McGill? Oh! She was looking forward so much to the trip. What happened?"

She rummaged in her handbag for her

reading glasses but Martin impatiently whipped the note from her hand and read,

"UNABLE TO MAKE THE TRIP MOTHER SUFFERED STROKE EARLY THIS MORNING."

"How dreadful for her," said Flora but a flush stealing up her neck revealed her anxiety. It was as if she had said, 'and what of me?'

Martin's fingers tapped steadily on the bedside table then stopped abruptly. "Do you realize what this means?" he asked, looking straight at her. "You will be absolutely alone all the way. Will you be able to manage?"

"Of course! I'll be fine!" she whispered, but her hands shifting backwards and forwards along the top of her handbag belied her confident words. Martin knew she was terrified.

He looked down at his shoes as if studying the specks of dust. There was nothing he could do at this late hour and of this Flora was well aware. At least he had tipped the steward generously. His conscience was clear. And if something happened to Flora would that not suit his plans admirably? He dismissed the new development from his mind with his customary directness and stood up, crumpling the message in his hand, then with an air of finality he threw it into the waste paper basket.

"Well! Let's take a look around, shall we?" he suggested and guided Flora firmly before him out of the cabin and through the milling throng before she could panic. Unfortunately everyone seemed to be taking a look around at the same time and they were jostled and pushed by excited passengers and their equally excited friends, until they were forced to seek refuge in the lounge. They found two hard-backed chairs and for some while sat uneasily watching the foremost crane hoisting last-minute cargo. There had never been much idle conversation between them and Martin was beginning to feel the strain of silently waiting. It was past sailing time. He turned to his wife.

"Everything is spotless, isn't it?" he murmured politely.

Flora nodded absentmindedly and he saw she was on the edge. She will be better when they cast off, I'm sure, he thought. And so shall I!

"I hope it won't be too rough," he added stiffly.

"It won't matter; I'm a good sailor."

I suppose she is, he thought, mildly surprised that for some twenty years he had not known this simple fact. What else is there to learn about my wife, he wondered. A good deal, most probably, but he was not interested. He had borne with her for his own reasons and she had been too stupid to understand but his daughter, perhaps, had understood. There was nothing of her mother in her!

Beth had always been a bright child and had grown to be a lovely, intelligent, young lady who had seemed to know instinctively what Martin thought and what he wished of her. Often they would sit together in complete harmony, not feeling the need to chatter as their thoughts wove invincible strands around them and when finally words invaded their cocoon of silence, it was to find each had been thinking along similar lines. 'On the same wavelength' Martin would say, and they would laugh together. Beth had asked him once if one could hate with one's body as one could love. It had been a surprising question for a fifteen-year-old girl and it had thrown him momentarily off balance, but he had wondered then if perhaps she understood him as no one else ever would.

Flora's voice jerked him to the present.

"Please remind Jackson to water my indoor plants."

"Oh! Yes, of course! And if you need money, or anything else for that matter, just telegraph me, but I suppose you will have enough for the few weeks on board."

"I should think so. I won't need much."

"And for goodness' sake don't lose your passport!"

"I'll take care. Don't worry."

They lapsed again into unhappy silence. Flora's restless fingers were now opening and closing her handbag. Click-clack. Click-clack. Somehow Martin restrained the impulse to shout at her.

"Please don't wait," she said, rising abruptly as if she knew his jagged mood. "The cranes have stopped now. We'll be sailing soon and you may be needed at the hospital."

Martin nodded, glad of the excuse, and together they made their way toward the gangplank.

"Good-bye," she said, her voice uncertain.

"Good-bye, Flora. I'll be over in a few weeks."

He leaned forward and lightly kissed her cheek. He noticed that the scent of gardenias was almost more overpowering than that of brandy. For an instant he wondered why he had bothered to kiss her. Whom was he fooling — Flora, himself or the world? Then he hurried down on to the dock, his mind already busy with preparations for his brief spell with Anthea.

A southeaster had sprung up and was blowing fiercely, whipping the sea into millions of white horses. *Fengu Girl* strained at her moorings while busy seamen darted about preparing to cast off. The tugs stood by, churning up the water and hooting their strident messages from time to time. Passengers leaned over the rails, waving and calling to friends. There was an air of gaiety and excitement but Flora stood quietly alone, her eyes following Martin as he walked away along the dock. He did not turn to wave. With head bent against the wind, clutching his hat with one hand and with his trousers winding around his thin legs as the gusts caught them, he rounded a corner and disappeared from her sight.

Some twenty minutes later, as Martin drove along De Waal Drive to the hospital and Anthea, he looked down. The tiny vessel, now left to her fate by the noisy tugs, was fighting to hold her course in the choppy seas beyond the breakwater. As he watched a grin spread slowly across his face.

"Yes, Lizzie! You could very well be right! The sea will be bad luck for her I'm sure!" he murmured.

7

FLORA clutched her wide-brimmed hat with one hand, her bulky handbag with the other, and pressed close to the rail as the wind tore at her tent-like coat, flapping it noisily against her legs. Her new shoes pinched her feet. Her new brassiere pressed into her flesh. She felt thoroughly uncomfortable and close to tears.

Slowly she went down to her cabin. There was no one about. Locking the door after her, she angrily kicked off her high-heeled shoes, threw her hat on to the berth and hitched her underwear into a more comfortable position.

"So much for my fancy outfit!" she muttered. "I could have worn rags for all he cared! And that damned hat!"

She knelt beside one of the small suitcases and fumbled about among her clothing. In a few seconds she found what she had been looking for — a slim brandy flask. She gulped a few mouthfuls, wiped her lips on the back of her hand and replaced the flask. Then she sat back on her heels. That was better! She was glad Miss McGill had not come. She might have been good company but she undoubtedly would have spied on her.

"I can do as I please! I'm free!" she cried, striking a dramatic pose before the mirror, arms high, feet well apart. She laughed and her image laughed back at her, but suddenly the note of gaiety was gone. The laughter died away slowly. Her hands dropped to her sides. She stood silently before her reflection while through the porthole came the dim sounds of departure. Her lips quivered. Quickly she turned away and began rummaging again in her suitcase. She brought out a head scarf and a pair of flat-heeled walking shoes, put them on and made her way back to the deck. She was aware that *Fengu Girl* had left her moorings but was amazed to find her already half way through the narrow channel to the sea. She found a vacant place against the rail and looked down. Scores of people lined the concrete pier, waving and cheering as the vessel sailed past. Streamers, released from outstretched hands, snaked through the air and were swiftly borne across the wharf or sank from sight beneath the white-tipped waves.

Soon they were in open water and the full strength of the wind struck the ship as she swung around, spray bursting in intermittent showers onto the deck. The passengers left hurriedly to take shelter, but Flora remained watching the huge waves sweeping toward them and the vessel rising to meet them time and again, as if overcoming her troubles one by one. She was drenched. Wisps of damp hair strayed from under her wet scarf and blew into her eyes, but she turned her face invitingly to the wind. The salty tang on her lips brought nostalgic memories of a girl sailing around the rugged coast of Scotland with her father and brothers. She had been young and happy then and life had held great promise. Now, at just forty, she felt old, disillusioned and alone. A tear trickled down her cheek and mingled with the salt spray.

"He didn't even turn to wave!" she murmured to the crying seagulls. Was he thinking already of Anthea? Was she, after all, important to him? Had this voyage been arranged to leave him free to pursue her for weeks? If so, why? Martin had been perfectly free to come and go without question, for it was well known that medical expertise could be required at any time of the day or night.

When Martin first planned this holiday, Flora had hoped it might be some effort on his part to bring them together, but she should have known better. Over the years they had been close for only a brief time when his parents were killed. He had needed her then, needed her love and warmth, but her big mistake was in thinking he loved her. A girl in love with him was but a boost to his ego. When she realized that her hold over him was fast disappearing she panicked. She told him that she was pregnant.

"My God!" he had shouted. "This NOW, when I'm in the middle of exams. Well! I don't want any child of mine done away with or branded a bastard! You'd better arrange something! A Registry Office I suppose, and make it soon!"

It was months later before Martin discovered that their baby was born well after Flora's expected date of delivery. He was furious.

"You lied to me!" he stormed. "Was it the thought of all that money I'd inherited from my parents? You're just a scheming little bitch! I'll make you pay for this thing you've done to me!"

Flora had cringed with shame then and now, so many years later, a flush crept up her neck at the thought.

"Well! It never was much of a marriage," she sighed. A happy brood of children would have given her a family to turn to, to work for, but Beth was the only one and she was so like her father!

Flora felt uneasy, but whether it was a premonition or merely subconscious jealousy she did not know.

"If only there was someone I could talk to," she murmured. She knew only too well that Martin never did anything without a good reason. What then was his motive for this holiday, the first they had taken together in over ten years? Icy tentacles of disquiet seemed to reach out to touch her. She shivered.

Cape Town, with Table Mountain as a backdrop, greyed to a hazy blur and gradually faded from view as *Fengu Girl* sailed north. Chilled and taut from the cold, Flora turned slowly away. It was dusk and she should think about going down to dinner, but she was not hungry and did not feel like facing strangers.

She unpacked her bags then soaked in a hot bath until the cold left her. Warm and refreshed she slipped into her nightgown and robe and climbed onto her bunk to look out. Through the porthole she could see isolated lights twinkling on the distant land. The vessel was still ploughing through heavy seas but the wind had died to a stiff breeze.

There was a sharp tap on the door.

"Come in!" she called.

The steward entered with a tray.

"I saw you were not at dinner, Mrs. Nolan. Are you feeling all right?"

"Oh! I'm fine, thanks," Flora answered. "I'm just tired. All the excitement I think."

"I've brought you a little beef-tea and toast but if you would like dinner I'll see if I can get some for you."

"That is kind of you, but I'm not hungry really. The beef-tea and toast will be just right."

"Well — if you don't feel too good during the night, please ring for me. There's a heavy swell running."

"Thanks, but it shouldn't bother me. I've always been an excellent sailor, though oddly enough I can't swim!"

The steward looked at her a moment and then smiled.

"I can go one better than that, Mrs. Nolan. I'm an old man now. I've spent forty-five years at sea and I've never learned to swim, though I'd rather you kept that to yourself, please!"

Flora laughed heartily. "Well! For both our sakes I certainly hope *Fengu Girl* doesn't sink."

"Oh, I'm sure she won't," he answered readily. "She's a strong, muscular girl, I'm sure. You can rest easy!"

"Incidentally, I've never heard of a Fengu girl. Is that an African name?"

"Yes. I understand the Fengu tribe live in the eastern part of the Cape Province. They are neighbours of the Xhosa people, who also wear red ochre clothing. You should talk to the Captain about the Fengus. He lived nearby when he was a boy."

"That's interesting. I'd like to talk to him some time."

The steward nodded and turned to go. "I'd better be getting along now. Good night."

"Good night, Steward."

When he left the cabin Flora dipped a piece of toast into the hot beef-tea and then into her mouth. It was good of the old man to think of her. He seemed kind and thoughtful and she was glad he was around.

For some time that night she tossed around in her bunk, the unaccustomed noises and her turbulent thoughts at first keeping her wakeful, but at last she fell asleep lulled by the soothing sound of quieting waves lapping rhythmically against the hull.

* * *

The next morning Flora rose early. She dressed carefully, put on her make-up and went down to breakfast, eager now to get the ordeal over of meeting her fellow passengers, but there was no one about. She saw on the seating plan that a place had been allotted to her and as she sat down she wondered whether she had come too early or whether there was another room set aside for breakfast. She was about to leave when a table steward appeared.

"I'm so sorry!" he said apologetically, hurrying over and holding the menu before her.

"Where is everyone this morning?" Flora asked.

"They are sleeping late, I imagine. Probably they're not very interested in the thought of eggs and bacon," he added with a big smile.

"But don't people take pills these days if they are poor sailors?" she asked.

"Most of them do, I think, but the heavy rolling and pitching yesterday were too much for some, pills and all!"

"Really? I'm luckier than the others, then."

Flora ordered her breakfast and had just picked up her glass of grapefruit juice when a stocky man in uniform entered. He looked around him and then at Flora. She smiled diffidently as he stopped opposite her chair.

"Good morning, Captain."

"A good morning it certainly is, now that I have a lovely lady to talk to!" he said with a great flourish of gallantry. Clear blue eyes twinkled at her as he sat down opposite her, then he looked serious.

"You must be Mrs. Martin Nolan."

Flora nodded.

"I heard you were to be one of the passengers this trip. My sister is a staff nurse at Groote Schuur. She knows your husband well and often works for him."

"Oh!"

There was silence. Flora could think of nothing to say that might be of interest. She knew the Captain was still looking at her and felt ill at ease. She wondered how much he had heard about Martin and their life together.

"Will you be in Canada long?" he asked.

"About a month. My husband is flying over later. We are to visit our daughter and meet our new grandchild."

"Grandchild! You must have married very young!"

Flora smiled shyly. "I suppose I did."

"Is this your first voyage?" he asked, moving the cutlery further apart in front of him.

"No. When I was in my late teens I left Great Britain on the first leg of a working tour to Australia. As you will realize, I didn't get far. Cape Town to be exact!"

He laughed. "And that was where you married?"

Flora smiled. "Yes. And where is your home?"

"Bellville, but *Fengu Girl* plies between Montreal and Lourenco Marques, so I'm at sea most of the time."

He twirled the salt and pepper pots on the cloth before him, then he spoke quietly, as if to himself.

"Fancy leaving an attractive wife to travel alone! Isn't your husband afraid of losing you?"

Flora laughed. "Oh, no! Such a possibility wouldn't enter his head!"

"These dedicated men never seem to

see further than their noses, do they? You'll have to give him something to think about, won't you?"

His voice was low, suggestive, with a hint of laughter. He leaned forward to pick up the menu and Flora felt his gaze linger on her low-cut neckline. She felt herself flushing and discovered her hands were suddenly clammy. She smiled awkwardly and the Captain threw back his head and roared at her discomfort.

Flora laughed too. It seemed the only thing to do. He was a 'lady-killer' most definitely, but she liked him.

She bent over her food and cast a covert glance in his direction. His hair was sandy, almost ginger, and his face florid, peppered with freckles. His shoulders were massive, his hands large and covered with hair that gleamed gold in the morning sunlight falling in shafts across the small table. The muscles in his strong neck stood out in cords as he turned his head.

"And I haven't even introduced myself!" he said. "I'm Jock McPherson. It's a real Scots name, but I was born in South Africa — Camp's Bay."

"That's where we live! Isn't it a gorgeous place?"

"I suppose it is, but it can be most unpleasant when the wind blows."

"Yes, but on a calm, sunny day it's hard to beat. We have a house on the side of the mountain overlooking the sea. I love it. I don't go out much and the view means a great deal to me. I sit for hours watching the ships coming and going. I should have been a man! I'd have run away to sea!"

A wistful note had crept unbidden into her voice and Flora realized the Captain was looking at her, but she kept her eyes averted.

"I can't live without the sea," he said. "It's my whole life! I wouldn't change anything about it, though I do get lonely at times. I love my new ship too — the line of her, every nut and bolt. It was love at first sight, and when I saw her name I knew she was meant for me. You see, I lived in the Transkei for years when I was young. The Fengu girls, when they reached marriageable age, would bare their breasts. I thought that was a lovely idea, for they were beautiful to me, just as my boat seems lovely. Sometimes I can scarcely believe my luck at being appointed Captain, but then I'm not sure it is luck. I'm a firm believer in Henley's words:

> 'I am the master of my fate,
> I am the captain of my soul.'

"I usually get what I want!" His words seemed to have a hidden meaning. Flora glanced up questionably and caught the expression in his eyes. She rose quickly to hide the tell-tale flush that had sprung to her cheeks.

"Excuse me. I must go now," she muttered and pushing back her chair she fled, conscious that the Captain's eyes were following her every step. As she reached the doorway she heard a soft chuckle. For an instant her footsteps faltered, then she sped quickly on.

8

ON reaching her cabin Flora closed the door behind her and stood leaning against it, furious that she had acted like a schoolgirl when she should have been coldly sophisticated and able to converse with sparkle and wit. The Captain had enjoyed baiting her and she, stupidly, had let him see how dull-witted she had become. She realized that being alone so much in recent years had left its mark. Having a man take an interest in her, even in fun, after all those years had caught her off balance. She recognized only too well that the Captain, like most sailors, probably made advances to every woman he met. She had no delusions about him in that respect, yet she remained strangely disturbed by his behaviour.

For some time she wandered restlessly around her cabin, then ran cold water into the hand basin and bathed her burning cheeks. Carefully patting them dry she walked over to the mirror and looked searchingly at herself. Tired eyes (somewhat faded, she thought) stared back at her. She leaned forward to remove a smudge of mascara, added a touch of lipstick to her lips and sighed. At least her figure was still good, she decided. She turned to the left and then to the right, noting her rigid abdominal muscles, and started to feel more cheerful.

Presently she picked up a pile of magazines and curled up on her berth with them, but her mind kept wandering to the Captain. She turned pages automatically for some while, but at last truth dawned in a sudden moment of clarity. She was not disturbed by the Captain's behaviour but by her own! The idea of being close to him intrigued her. It had been a long, lonely time since she had felt strong arms around her. She went over and over in her mind what she would say to him, imagining what he might say to her. The fact that he might, perhaps, not pursue her further never entered her mind.

When the ship's bell summoned her to lunch, she tidied herself and made her way toward the dining saloon, but then her courage failed her. She turned away, entered the deserted bar lounge and sat down on the nearest leather stool.

"Brandy. Just a dash of soda, please," she said. "Make it a double while you are about it, will you?"

The steward was too well trained to show his surprise. Quietly he set the brandy down in front of her. Flora sat looking at it, then she began to smile. It really was amusing. She was hungry, yet reluctant to go into lunch in case the Captain was there! She could not starve all the way to Canada! She giggled, then stopped short as she caught sight of the bar steward's expression.

"It's all right," she laughed. "I'm not crazy or tipsy, only thinking! Can you have a drink with me? I usually have to drink alone and I hate it."

"Thanks," he answered, "but I'd better not while I'm on duty. The Captain wouldn't like that one bit! He'd probably skin me alive!" and he smiled.

Flora smiled back.

"Does he often get mad?" she asked.

He thought for a moment.

"No. I can't say he does," he said. "We have our duties and we know the rules. I don't think we'd try to do anything he would not approve of. He's a good captain and what he says goes, that's all!"

Flora nodded. "Have you known him long?"

"Well! I'd say close on ten years now. We were together on a small freighter for a while, and when he was given command of this steamer I transferred. A couple of us did. The Captain arranged it. We're a happy crew. It's a good life."

Flora twirled her glass thoughtfully around on the counter. She wanted to know if the Captain had a girl in every port, but felt she had shown too much interest in him already.

"I hear our first port is Luanda," she said, to change the subject.

"Not this time," he answered. "We are making a brief stop at Walvis Bay first — some special shipment for the Canadian Government I understand."

"Shall we be allowed on shore?"

"Not until we reach Luanda and then

again at Las Palmas on Gran Canaria."

"Where is that?"

"One of the Canary Islands."

"Of course! I haven't been there. The ship called at Madeira when I was on my way to South Africa many years ago."

The steward nodded politely.

"The Captain arranges tours for the passengers if they are interested," he said. "You should let him know."

"Thank you. I shall."

He bent down to dust the glasses on a low shelf behind the counter, and Flora realized she had kept him from his work. She finished her brandy and feeling more composed walked into the dining saloon. The Captain's chair was empty, and for a moment she could not decide whether she felt disappointed or relieved.

Taking the seat she had occupied at breakfast, she nodded to the few passengers who were apparently feeling better and noticed she was the only female amongst them. She made a quick assessment and decided there were no possible friends for her here. Unless she did something about this depressing situation, the voyage to Canada would be but a continuation of her lonely life with Martin. She looked around her.

On her left sat a grubby-looking, middle-aged man with an untidy head of woolly black hair, thick horn-rimmed spectacles and bushy beard. He seemed to be eating everything put before him with great determination, never raising his eyes from his plate. His beard was lightly spattered with traces of vermicelli. Flora turned away wishing that he had been seated elsewhere. Across the table to her right a lanky young man in a shabby but clean sports jacket caught her eye. He grinned boyishly at her and the well-scrubbed look of her brother Jamie as a schoolboy made her grin back at him. Two empty feeding bottles stood like sentinels on the table before him.

"I presume you have babies to feed," she said, indicating the bottles. "Is it one or two?"

The young man pulled off a piece of bread roll and chewed slowly at it before he answered.

"One of three months and one of twenty-one months," he drawled. "Some voyage this will be, I can tell you!

Twenty-six days and twenty-six nights! Long dreary nights they'll be for sure! If one kid isn't howling the other is! But we adore them all the same!"

Flora's heart went out to him. He looked so young to be the father of two. Suddenly she knew what she must do to occupy her mind and time.

"I'll be glad to help out sometimes," she said. "I love babies. Would your wife trust me with them?"

The young man's face broke into a smile.

"Sure she would! Gosh! We'd be mighty grateful if you would take over once in a while."

"Well. Tell your wife I'll be along to see her before the children's supper tonight. I could take the bigger one in to his meal while she feeds the baby or perhaps sit with them both while you and your wife go to dinner. What number is your cabin?"

"No. 2. Oh, thanks! That will give us a real break! I feel better already."

Flora smiled. She felt happy at the thought of something to do and looked forward to being with the children.

About 5:30 that evening Flora began her unofficial duties as mother's help, for in the days that followed two more children were tucked under her wing from time to time. She found great joy in the mothers' need of her and in the children's warm and spontaneous demonstrations of affection, the chubby arms held out so trustingly, the toothless baby smiles.

Flora was scarcely aware of the vessel's stop in Walvis Bay and that evening, on returning to her cabin, the fragrance of roses greeted her. She switched on the light and gazed in amazement at the arrangement of dark roses that had been placed upon the dressing table. Quickly she opened the envelope that was propped against the bowl.

'Forgive me,' the note read. 'I didn't mean to frighten you away! I've been in to meals early and late but I've missed you every time. Please try to join me for a nightcap before you go to bed. I'll be free at ten tonight. Will you meet me in the bar lounge? Please don't disappoint me.
Jock.
P.S. I do hope you like the roses.'

Flora smiled as she glanced at her wrist watch. There was almost an hour. That would give her plenty of time. She bent her head towards the flowers, then held out her hand to cup a bloom. It was a perfect bud, its proud head resting on a long, straight stem, the soft velvety petals folded one upon the other as if protecting an inner loveliness still to be revealed. Her eyes grew misty. She felt a tenderness in her heart as though touched by a warm and gentle hand.

She took great pains with her appearance, and as she entered the lounge she was rewarded by the Captain's appraising look. She knew her purple dress was striking and was delighted he seemed to like it. He rose smiling as she approached, and Flora felt she was seeing a good friend, yet their last meeting had been brief and had ended with her running away. A few days of missing him, and a bowl of roses, had worked their magic.

"So you came! Now I know you've forgiven me," he said, holding out his hands to take hers.

"There was nothing to forgive. You were just being your usual self, I suppose, but I was not used to you," she said smiling.

He laughed loudly and the bridge players in the opposite corner peered interestedly in their direction. Flora hastily took her seat.

"What would you like to drink?"

"Brandy and soda, please," she answered and realized with a start that she had scarcely had a drink since she took on her 'babies.' She had been completely occupied and happy. There had been no need to drown her sorrows, no need to blot out the frightening cold in Martin's eyes. Martin! Where was he now? she wondered. With Anthea? She felt chilled but she stifled her unhappy thoughts and turned to her companion with a show of brightness.

"I haven't thanked you for the flowers," she said. "They are simply gorgeous! The cabin is filled with their scent."

"I'm pleased you like them. I radioed through to a friend in Customs in Walvis Bay. He arranged for them to be sent to his office for me so I did not have to go right into town. I wasn't even missed!"

"That was clever of you!"

A little thought nagged at Flora. Was this the usual procedure? Was there always someone on board for the Captain to indulge? She thrust the unwelcome thought from her mind. What did it really matter? It was the present that was important, not the hateful past nor the uncertain future.

The Captain splashed a little soda into Flora's glass. "Say when," he said.

"When!" she said almost immediately and gave an embarrassed laugh.

He smiled at her, then held up her glass.

"That was a drop in the ocean!" he said. "Why don't you drink your brandy neat, as I do? There is nothing like it!" and handed it to her. "Cheers!"

"Cheers!"

Their glasses met but Flora was careful not to meet his eyes. They twinkled in jest but missed nothing, she felt sure. What would he think if she told him she often dispensed with the soda, not to mention the glass? She must see that she did not drink too much in front of him. She took a small sip but she felt dishonest and it troubled her. She rushed into speech like a child covering up a lie, saying the first thing that came to mind.

"Er — tell me. Tell me about your life, yourself."

There was a moment's silence. The Captain stubbed idly with a cigarette butt in the ashtray before him, and finally he spoke.

"There isn't much to tell, I'm sorry to say. Life at sea may be rather monotonous for some adventurous fellows, but I'm a lazy chap. I enjoy the orderly, unhurried way of life, the tranquillity of calm sailing, with the occasional challenge of a storm or mishap to keep me on my toes. But I don't want to talk about myself! I want to know about you!"

He sat back and raised his glass to his lips as Flora looked up. She studied his face seriously and suddenly he smiled.

"I'm really rather a nice person!"

She laughed and picked up her brandy.

"Now, that's better!" He shifted his position then rose and moved over to sit beside her.

"I suppose you are excited at the thought of seeing your daughter."

Flora turned slightly to be able to look at him. "Yes. I haven't seen her for almost two years and she's our only child. But I'm scared too. Will she be as glad to see me?"

She ran her fingers restlessly along the top of the beaded handbag, aghast at herself. This last question had slipped out quite by accident, like a drop of mercury from a cracked thermometer. She had not meant to bare those secret little fears to a comparative stranger. She knew it was something one did not do. Martin would not have approved. He would have sent her a withering look if he could have heard her but (and she had almost forgotten) he was many miles away. She could be herself for once, say exactly what she wished, when and how she wished! The Captain would understand, of that she felt certain. She plunged headlong on.

"You see, Beth and I never saw eye to eye about anything ever! If I liked something white, she liked it black, especially if she knew that was the way her father wanted it. She will probably be worse now. She is married to a real snob and she thinks he is just wonderful. He's a bigwig in the oil business and has definite views he likes to air. I find him frightening. He is very superior in his own eyes and makes me feel so ignorant. I say all the wrong things when he is around. I simply dread meeting him again."

Flora crumpled a tissue into a tight ball and straightened it carefully again before she continued. He sat quietly looking at her, but his eyes were kind. Flora knew that she had a sympathetic listener.

"I can hear Arthur apologizing for his mother-in-law when I'm gone," she went on. "I shall not mind so much, but what I'm most afraid of is that Beth will be ashamed of me too."

Jock leaned forward across the small table and looked straight into her eyes.

"What nonsense!" he said softly. "You underestimate your true worth. I scarcely know you, but it did not take me long to realize you are loving, generous and kindhearted. Surely those qualities count for something."

"I suppose so," Flora whispered. She drained her glass quickly and smiled weakly at him.

"I'm sorry! I didn't mean to burden you with my silly fears."

"I'm glad you felt you could talk to me," he said. "I like to be needed and if it helps at all I think you are an absolute honey. I've heard how you are helping with the children and as the Captain I am most grateful. We don't usually have such young kiddies on board, and it's hard on the parents with no proper facilities. As a friend, let me say that if your family doesn't appreciate you, they need their heads read!"

Flora put out her hand impulsively and pressed his fingers briefly.

"Thank you," she said, almost inaudibly. "I needed that!" Her lips quivered. She tried to say more, but could not. She made a move to go, but the Captain put a detaining hand on her arm.

"Don't go yet, please! The coffee urn is still on. Let's have a cup."

Flora hesitated. Another drink was what she needed but perhaps the coffee would do just as well.

"That's a good idea," she said, biting on her lip to keep from crying. "Shall I help you to get it?"

"Oh, no thanks. You sit just where you are. If the ship makes a sudden move the urn is apt to turn nasty and spit. I'd hate you to burn yourself." Smiling, he left her.

The tears that suddenly welled up threatened to fall, but she quickly dabbed them away with a tissue. She groped for her powder compact, but there was no time to use it before the Captain returned bearing a small tray. Flora kept her eyes down.

"Well! Here we are!" he said cheerfully. "I had to coax that old urn, but I managed to squeeze a few drops out of her."

Out of the corner of her eye Flora saw him looking intently at her as if trying to assess her mood. He bustled about with the coffee cups, keeping up a ceaseless chatter, and she was grateful to him. He was doing his best to cheer her, but she was not really listening. She could think only of the lonely, meaningless years that stretched ahead of her and of her need for a stiff drink.

She sipped the coffee slowly and then,

without warning her hands began to shake.

The bridge four in the opposite corner of the room rose at that moment. They nodded on their way out and Flora absentmindedly nodded back. The Captain wished them all a good night and then he and Flora were alone. In the stillness she struggled to keep her cup from rattling in its saucer. The Captain quietly took them away from her and set them on the table. Moving to the arm of her chair he took her hands in his and held them firmly, comfortingly.

"I do hate to see you so sad," he said softly. "You shouldn't be, you know. You have so much to be happy about, so much to be grateful for. Everything is going to be just fine with that son-in-law of yours too. You'll see! And you're going to have a wonderful holiday, the best you have ever had! It's going to start right now! I'll see to that personally!"

He put his head on one side and grinned. "Now let's take a turn around the deck. The exercise will do us both good," he said firmly, and rose, pulling Flora to her feet. She did not resist and in a short while had regained control of herself. On the upper deck, with her wrap snugly around her shoulders and her arm tucked into the strong, muscular one of her companion, she stepped briskly along, listening to Jock's gay chatter and feeling strangely at peace. But presently their footsteps became less brisk and they fell silent, as though their idle talk and laughter shattered the complete harmony.

Suddenly, with an abruptness that was startling, the moon sailed from behind a cloud, causing them with one accord to pause as if to imprint the loveliness on their minds. Flora was suddenly aware of Jock's nearness, the feel of his jacket, the touch of his hand, his warm breath against her cheek. He drew her quietly and gently around to face him. As his arms enfolded her she felt a deep sense of belonging. She raised her face to his.

9

AFTER days of turbulence that had seemed never-ending, the wind abated and *Fengu Girl* slid at last through a tranquil sea with scarcely a ripple, as though tired now of performing her tricks, her nose pointing doggedly north as she hugged the west coast of Africa.

Flora felt happier than she had been for years, fitting contentedly into her particular niche in the overall mosaic of passengers and crew. Always ready with a gentle smile, she became quite a favourite on board and was grateful for their warm companionship. Even the middle-aged man on her left in the dining saloon had proved to be gentle, highly intelligent and surprisingly full of humour. It still appeared as though he grew his beard especially as a repository for food tidbits, but he was delightfully amusing about it, blaming his old spectacles for causing the problem.

The days were filled with activity, with her 'children' primarily, but Flora still managed a game of deck quoits or Scrabble with the adults from time to time. In the evenings she would slip away to her cabin and rest quietly and read. Her old steward had got into the habit of bringing her milk and biscuits about 9 p.m. and she looked forward to his visits. He would sit on a chair near the door for a while to chat comfortably with her about his family that he saw so seldom and of his many adventures at sea. She, in turn, would tell him about her childhood or her proposed visit to Beth in Canada and the grandchild who was expected at any time now. Then, when the old man had gone, she would read a while longer as she waited for Jock. Sometimes he was unable to get away but when he did they would sit companionably together, holding hands like teenagers, or perhaps they would make love. He had become all-important to her, and she kept a firm reign on herself so that he would not suspect it, but as the days passed it became more and more difficult for her.

At Luanda Flora stayed on board with the children. The stifling heat and surging crowds on shore had suddenly seemed menacing, but by the time they sailed into the picturesque harbour of Las Palmas, she felt a great need to walk on solid earth again. When Jock proposed to drive her around the island to see the sights, she was as excited as a child and promised to be ready early.

Soon after breakfast the following morning most of the passengers climbed into taxis. Flora stood patiently on deck, gazing at the pastel shades of the small houses dotted around and up the hillside. It was a bright, windless day and she felt like a young girl as she wiggled her bare toes inside her open sandals and tied a scarf around her sunhat and under her chin. She was used to waiting, for Jock had made it clear to her from the outset that his ship must come first and that sometimes there were problems to solve.

Flora was looking idly around when suddenly there was a great cheering and tooting on shore, coming ever closer and louder. Soon a dilapidated car of ancient vintage drew to a halt before the gangway, disgorging several youngsters all yelling and laughing at once at the obvious joy of their unexpected ride.

The driver alighted, looked up at her and waved.

"Hi there!"

Flora could not believe her eyes. It was Jock, dressed in a pair of white shorts, an old T-shirt and a floppy hat, festooned with artificial daisies and purple grapes.

She burst out laughing as she ran down to join him.

"Jock! You're priceless!" she laughed, "And wherever did you find that hat?"

He smiled.

"I knew you'd love it! It wasn't even for sale! I just showed the toothless old gal wearing it a fistful of money and the next thing it was mine!"

That was the start of a day of laughter and warmth. They walked barefoot along the beach with old-fashioned bathing tents dotted in clusters like brightly coloured toadstools, they mingled with the workers on a coffee plantation and, with much fun and shrieks of joy, were jolted off the backs of two scrawny, bored-looking camels. They climbed on the rim of a crater to look down on a small farm nestling in the centre and threw coins to the young children playing outside their cave homes, where washing festooned the landscape and goats clambered sure-footed along the steep hillside.

At lunch time Jock produced a hamper of sandwiches, fruit and a bottle of local wine, which they consumed on a lonely beach, watching the lazy breakers, reluctant to move on.

Later they rose to drive to their final stop where they knelt together, two tourists among the colourful islanders singing and praying in the old cathedral where Christopher Columbus prayed for guidance before setting out on his historic voyage westward. To Flora it seemed as if she too were setting sail to a new land, a land of the unknown, and a chill stole through her. She moved closer to Jock to feel his nearness and was comforted, but all too soon it was time for their return to the little ship. She knew now that every minute of every hour would have to be counted and stored in her treasury of memories, for when they again set sail they would be heading in a north-westerly direction toward the vast land that was Canada. Jock's almost constant vigilance would be needed for the perhaps hazardous Atlantic crossing with its mountainous seas and piercing cold winds.

Seated beside Jock in the ancient car she knew that she loved him. Often in their tender moments she had longed to tell him, but a foolish pride held her back. He had never said he loved her. He had always been attentive and loving but she knew he was too honest to lie to her. She was forced to face reality. Their relationship was to him merely that of a shipboard affair. He had never spoken of his home life and she had never dared to ask, afraid to hear him speak of his wife and children, afraid perhaps to see a soft gleam of love in his eyes at the mention of them.

Flora remembered the first time she was invited to his cabin. A pretty young woman and two small boys had gazed at her from a leather frame on the desk. Tactfully she had not referred to the photograph and on her next visit it was not there.

Now she looked up at him as he drove along the narrow, dusty road. He had promised her the best holiday ever and it had been even more than that. She put out her hand and touched his cheek lightly with her forefinger.

"I've been so happy," she said.

He took one hand from the wheel and pressed her fingers, then raised them to his lips and kissed them one by one.

"Flora, my dear!" he said and his eyes were suddenly damp and his voice had a tremor that was most unusual for him. She snuggled against his shoulder and did not speak until they neared the dock. It seemed that they were both sad as they climbed on board to change for dinner but soon the passengers returned full of enthusiasm and banter, and the mood of gloom that was threatening to engulf Flora mercifully dispelled.

Two days later, while Flora was reading

to two of her small charges, she received a radiogram.

"I hope it means good news for you, Mrs. Nolan," said the steward as he handed it to her.

"Oh, yes! I hope so too!" she answered, her thoughts at once on Beth.

Quickly she ripped open the envelope, unfolded the paper and started to read. Then she threw up her hands in joy.

"It's a boy! Seven pounds, two ounces!" she answered, hugging the children to her. "That calls for a celebration, doesn't it?"

The steward nodded.

"Congratulations! I'm so glad!" he said. "I'll see what can be done. How about a bottle or two of champagne and cake for tea?"

"Oh! Yippee!" shouted small Sandra, the elder of the two children. "Can we have tea right now?"

Flora and the steward roared with laughter.

"As soon as the cake is ready little one," said the steward, patting her on the head. Then he went happily off to spread the good news.

Flora put the children on a couch with the copy of *Cinderella* that she had been reading to them and again picked up the radiogram. It read:

'CONGRATULATIONS GRANDMOTHER STOP ARTHUR JAMES SEVEN POUNDS TWO OUNCES BORN TWO A.M. TUESDAY STOP BOTH WELL ALL HAPPY STOP SEE YOU SOON
LOVE MARTIN.'

She kept looking at the words for something about them worried her, but her good news was racing through the ship like a dry forest fire and before she knew it she was in the middle of a party with everyone hugging her and wishing her well.

Champagne, platters of hors d'oeuvres, and nuts appeared as though by magic and later, to the delight of the children, a cake was brought in by the chef himself. It was decorated and piped in blue and white icing with the words WELCOME TO BABY, and it brought a burst of applause from everyone. Smiling broadly, the chef raised his hands before him to gain a moment's silence and said, "This was destined for trifle tonight!" Everyone clapped and laughed and insisted that he join them in a glass of champagne.

The merrymaking stretched well into the dinner hour. By the time it ended Flora and many of the passengers were rather unsteady on their feet, not entirely due to the rough sea, and when Flora escaped eventually to seek refuge in her cabin she climbed into her bunk exhausted.

"Jock! Oh! Jock!" she whispered. "Why can't you come?"

He had sent word that he would be unable to join in the festivities but she had missed him and now realized how difficult her life would be without him. She stared at the lines of pipes that straddled the low ceiling, but they refused to stay still. They waved into shapes like seaweed with faces that mocked her popping up between them. She closed her eyes but they did not go away.

Suddenly she sat bolt upright, her eyes wide with terror.

"Of course! Martin never in his life sent me love!" she moaned. "Why now? Is he trying to impress me or someone else?" She climbed out of her bunk, opened the low drawer in the dressing table and clutched at the brandy flask. And the words 'SEE YOU SOON!' she thought. Oh! No! She had almost forgotten. What if Martin found out about Jock? Her fingers clawed at the framework of the berth, the knuckles white from the strain.

"What have I done?" she moaned. "Oh! What have I done?"

She climbed back into the bunk still holding the flask firmly.

"Whatever can I do?" she asked the empty cabin. "Can I leave Martin before he discovers what I've done? But how?"

She rocked gently backwards and forwards, trying to marshall her thoughts and to plan. She had nothing of her own, except her clothing. She charged most of her purchases and Martin paid the bills. He had always insisted that she did not need her own bank account.

Yet how could she go back to that lifeless void that had been her life? One should never go back to anything on earth, for nothing ever remained completely static. Inevitably there are changes, no matter how subtle, that make a difference. Somehow she would have to go on. She had found a door that had opened a chink, just enough to show her another world beyond, but where would she find the strength and the means to pass through forever, to take her chances in the harsh world that beckoned? There could be no turning back.

"Maybe I'll have no choice!" she moaned. "Perhaps I'll be forced to make a move to the outside world and I'll have no help from anyone, certainly not from Martin or Beth and not now from Tom, who surely cared for me a little once, long ago, and perhaps now not even from Jock!"

She commenced to cry quietly, silently, and the tears poured down her cheeks unchecked.

The voyage was nearing its end and the happiness she had found with Jock would soon be over.

"Why can't we remain forever poised in time, stop the workings of time itself?" she asked herself. Soon there would be only memories, as always, but this time they would not be enough. There seemed no way out! She felt as if she had been painting a floor and had painted herself into a corner.

"Jock! Oh Jock!" she whispered. "Help me!" He had said he could not possibly slip away this evening, but it was now that she needed him desperately, needed his strong, comforting arms around her. She lay down again, but the pipes that straddled the ceiling still writhed in grotesque patterns, and Martin's cold, pale eyes seemed to be everywhere she looked, watching and waiting.

With a low moan she propped herself on to one elbow, opened the cap of the flask and with trembling hands held the container so that she could drink from it. Steadily she drank, but the eyes were everywhere. She could not escape them.

Presently there was a short, almost stealthy tap on the door. Quickly Flora wiped her mouth with her fingertips and attempted to screw the top back with one hand.

The tap came again.

"One moment!" she called, setting the flask down with the cap still off. Then, smoothing her hair, she walked over to the door, unlocked it and peeped out. The Captain stood outside. Flora opened the door wide and fell sobbing into Jock's arms. For a moment he held her close, then quietly he guided her inside, kicked the door shut and locked it.

"What is it, Flora, my dear?" he asked softly. "What has happened? Tell me."

But Flora could only sob and shake while he stroked her hair gently back from her forehead and rocked her like a child in his arms.

"I'm so scared!" she whispered, her eyes wild. "Oh! God! I'm so scared!"

She felt his arms tighten around her.

"What of? What is it my darling?"

Between half clenched teeth she said, "Martin! I'd quite forgotten! He's going to kill me!"

The captain laughed softly.

"Because of us, do you mean? My dear! What nonsense! He is probably just as guilty!" He drew her chin up to face his and kissed her lightly.

"You've been reading far too many trashy novels," he said. As he spoke he noticed the flask, with the cap lying beside it, on the bedside table.

Flora shook her head.

"You don't understand. He thinks he's some kind of a god. He can do whatever he pleases. And do you know something? He had me believing he can, too!"

Jock laughed. "Now you are being fanciful! He is only a man and not a very strong one at that! So relax, my love, relax!"

Flora looked up at him.

"I've been such a fool!" she said. "I always was and I haven't changed! Martin's been playing with me, like the storybook cat with his mouse. He's been waiting, just waiting, for this moment of triumph! This so-called holiday! I've suspected all along there was something wrong. He planned this trip for a reason. I know it now! I've been watching him closely for twenty years, remember, and he knows me too!"

She stopped and for a few moments they looked into each other's eyes. Then she continued.

"Martin is planning to kill me. I know that now. Whenever he hurt me in the past it was because of something I had done. He had to feel justified. Now it's the same thing. I've fallen right into his trap! He knew I'd do something foolish as soon as I didn't have his piercing eyes upon me. When he sees me he will read my guilt, even though he may not know what it is, and he'll feel justified in punishing me."

Jock held her more tightly for a moment, then he pulled her down with him onto her berth.

"This is nonsense! Utter and complete nonsense!" he said softly, dropping a kiss on her hair, but Flora did not seem to notice. She went on.

"He never wanted me after he found out I'd tricked him. You see, I had pretended I was pregnant so that he would marry me. When he found out that the baby was not due for another month, he was furious. I thought he'd kill me then! He threw me on the bed and stood staring at me, his face contorted with hatred. I was terrified and so cold. My teeth were chattering. At last he threw my gown over me. 'I want nothing more to do with you! NOTHING!' he said. 'Do you understand? You will be provided for as long as I wish, then I will make you pay for this thing that you have done to me!'"

Flora drew in her breath sharply.

"I've never told anyone this before," she said. "I couldn't. It was too private to talk about. But now, don't you see? The time has come for me to pay."

Jock patted her abstractedly, as if not knowing quite what to say and Flora went on.

"Martin is mad. I realise it now and there is nothing I can do about it — nothing at all! Who would believe ME, take MY word against his?"

Jock shifted uncomfortably in her arms and Flora clung to him as though afraid he might leave her.

"Martin knew I'd do something rash," she continued, "but he could not have foreseen that I'd fall in love, could he?"

She leaned back, the better to look into Jock's eyes, as if seeking reassurance from him.

Jock's eyes twinkled. "And have you fallen in love, me darlin'?" he teased.

Flora drew his head down to hers and held him close.

"You know only too well!" she answered softly.

Jock's breath caught in his throat and the air of banter vanished as he struggled to speak.

"Flora, my dear!" His words were almost inaudible. "There is something I must say — something I have to explain."

But Flora put a hand quickly over his mouth. "Don't! Please!" she said quietly. "There is no need. I know. There is your wife, and the children too. They love you and need you and always will, I suppose. I want nothing from you, nothing at all! Only that you will love me now a little and hold me close, very close! I want to forget — FORGET!"

10

FLORA had been gone for almost seven weeks when Martin parked his car on the sea front at Green Point and settled down to wait for Anthea. Out at sea the lights of passing ships winked gaily across the dark expanse of ocean and Martin was reminded of his forthcoming 'holiday' and the voyage home in the *S.S. Glenconnor*. His stomach contracted at the thought. Just a little more patience and he would be free of Flora forever, if all went well, but he was not certain that he had, as yet, made much progress with Anthea. She had always been ready and waiting to see him when their free evenings coincided, yet their eager lovemaking had left him strangely dissatisfied.

At first Anthea was reluctant to see him at her flat, so they would drive out of town to a motel or inn for a few hours of what she called 'debauchery,' which annoyed him. He wanted to hold her in his arms forever! He didn't care if the whole world knew about it. Her attitude was almost prudish, while he wanted to make love with no holds barred! Now apparently they were having difficulty finding any time together. He had a series of lectures to give on certain fixed evenings and Anthea's aunt and mother were arranging to come on a visit, especially to see her. Martin realized they were soon to be parted, and he was frankly unhappy. Did Anthea love him? Did she love him enough? These were questions that must be answered, for this would be, in all probability, their last outing together before he left for Canada.

His thoughts leaped eagerly ahead as if trying to beat the breakers that raced each other shorewards, their crests rippling ribbons of white in the darkness and he felt as restless as the snakes of seaweed swirling in cauldrons of foam beneath him.

"Damn!" he muttered. "Where is Anthea? Why doesn't she come?"

From time to time he glanced at the luminous dial on his watch and gradually his mood changed from impatience to anxiety. Anthea was late, later than she had ever been! Whatever could be keeping her? Alarmed, he switched the key in the ignition and was on the point of leaving to look for her when he saw a car turn off the road, its headlights sending jagged beams of light across the uneven ground as it came toward him. Martin opened his door and stepped out. The Volkswagen drew up beside him.

"Sweetheart! I thought you'd never come!" he said, helping Anthea out and taking her in his arms, but she pulled away from him.

"Don't please, Martin! Not here!" she said, tidying her hair.

"Why not? No one can see us."

Anthea did not reply. She climbed into the Mercedes-Benz and sat staring straight ahead. Martin looked at her in amazement, then slid in beside her.

"What is it?" he asked softly. "Is something the matter?"

She shook her head. "No, not really. Let's get away from here."

With a shrug Martin swung the car towards the road.

"Where shall we go tonight?" he asked brightly.

"Oh, anywhere! I don't care!" came the peevish reply.

Martin bristled.

"Well — as you don't seem interested, I don't propose to spend the whole night racing miles out of town and back again to make sure no one recognizes us. I had planned to take you to dinner in Somerset West. Now that's out of the question! You were very late, you know, and I didn't hear an apology!"

Anthea put her hands up to her face and Martin's ill-humour vanished instantly.

"My dear," he said. "Here we are on the verge of a quarrel, and all because of the most valued, precious moments I lost tonight."

He put out his hand and took hers and Anthea swung around and clung to him.

"Hey there!" he laughed. "That's not fair! I've got to concentrate on driving."

She sat up quickly.

"I'm sorry. I'm all mixed up these days. I can't go on like this. I'm having to lie to my friends about where I go and what I do and now — my mother! I wouldn't hurt her for the world, yet I did. I'm sure she suspects something. She asked a lot of questions when she telephoned today. I tried to hedge and finally told her to leave me alone and mind her own business! I don't know how I could have been so horrible!"

"Well! Well!" laughed Martin as he turned into a side street and stopped the car.

"You certainly have got yourself into a state, haven't you? You silly!" he said, as he held her close.

His sensitive fingers caressed her hair and gradually the tenseness seemed to leave her.

"Why don't you tell your mother that we love each other?" he asked. "If she knows that this is not just an idle affair — that I want to marry you one day — she'll get used to the idea."

"Don't talk like that, Martin!" retorted Anthea sharply, dabbing fiercely at her damp eyes with her handkerchief. "You know we can't ever get married. Flora would never let you go. You've said that many times. She's like a limpet clinging tightly to her rock and you are too mindful of a scandal to leave her. The whole situation is hopeless, so the fewer people who know about us the better. Well! You'll be gone in a few days. It'll be easier then. I'll just have to get a grip on myself and learn to live without you, but let's not talk about it now. We don't want to spoil our last evening together."

She put her hand up to his head and with her fingers traced his receding brow.

"I don't know what I see in you," she said smiling softly. "You are going bald, you have tired bags under your eyes and crow's feet, but I love you, or at least I think I do."

She drew his head toward her and kissed him. Martin's senses skyrocketed. She had never before kissed him like this! She had always seemed to be holding back and more than once he had felt thoroughly frustrated, his fleeting happiness clouded by doubt. But now he surrendered with joy to her unexpected warmth, hardly aware of the distant hum of traffic passing nearby with monotonous regularity.

Suddenly he tensed, conscious of a new sound. He drew quickly away from Anthea to find several Coloured urchins peering in at them, snickering behind their hands.

"Good grief!" Anthea exclaimed as she sat up. Then she began to laugh, but Martin was not amused. He shouted angrily through the car window.

"Haven't you anything better to do than to stand grinning?"

A burst of mocking laughter greeted his words and sent him into a rage.

"My God!" he muttered murderously as the youths began clamouring on to the car. Switching on the engine he drove off at high speed, dropping off the unwelcome passengers one by one. He knew Anthea was watching him but he was past caring.

"So you have got a temper after all!"

At her words, Martin forced a smile. He turned toward her but his eyes remained cold.

"I'm sorry," he answered. "Hooligans always upset me. I could cheerfully whip them!"

"You could have killed them too,

driving off like that! After all, it was our fault. We should not have given them cause to laugh at us. At any rate they sent us on our way. We might have sat all night under that street lamp."

Anthea was right, he thought. They should not have been displaying their feelings by the roadside. He must find a place where they could be alone. He headed toward Hout Bay and turned off the main street in the centre of the shopping centre.

"I've just had a brilliant idea," he said, bringing the car to rest beside a road house. The façade resembled the bow of an old sailing vessel. Young men in colourful pirate dress were taking orders as cars drew up under neon lights that flicked on and off — 'The Jolly Roger — Seafood our Specialty'.

Martin smiled across at Anthea, then flicked the car lights for service.

A young pirate stepped briskly forward.

"Good evening, sir."

"Two orders of lobster tails, mixed salad, hot rolls, and black coffee, please," Martin said and looked at Anthea for approval. She smiled and nodded.

"To take away, please."

"Right, sir."

Anthea laughed. "A picnic! So that's your brilliant idea!"

"Yes, at Llandudno. Let's drive over and watch the sea by moonlight."

Anthea turned towards him.

"And then?" she questioned.

Their eyes met and in those brief moments a score of questions seemed to flash between them. Martin drew her into his arms as a surge of emotion swept over him and they clung together.

"Oh, my darling. I don't know how I'm ever going to leave you," he murmured at last. "I wish now I'd never planned this trip."

"Your order, sir."

They broke quickly away, Martin scanned the bill and reached for his wallet. He allowed mentally for a good tip and counted out a few rand.

"You may keep the change."

"Thank you, Doctor."

Martin's hand, in the act of replacing his wallet, remained poised in mid-air.

"Good heavens! What did he say?" But the man had gone.

"Damn!" Martin spluttered. "I thought his face was familiar. He must be one of my students."

Anthea's hand flew to her mouth.

"Of course!" she said. "He is Jannie van Breda, the varsity scrum half. Well — it serves us right for playing with fire! My reputation as a loose woman is now undisputed!"

She threw up her hands in mock horror and started to laugh gaily. "Come on! Let's go! I'm starving!"

Martin could scarcely believe it. She was joking, yet a few minutes earlier she had been in tears at the thought of lying to her friends. He gave up the attempt to understand her unpredictable moods.

Within minutes they were on the mountain slope above Llandudno and Martin was steering the Mercedes down the narrow winding road to the cove. The moon had not yet risen and the stars seemed to shine with particular brilliance in the heavens. He felt strangely elated. Anthea was different tonight. He hoped this was significant. He smiled to himself.

"Why are you smiling?"

Martin turned in her direction but the light was dim. He laughed.

"How did you know I am?" he asked. "You can't possibly see my expression in the dark."

"I've got cat's eyes, that's how!" came the pat reply.

Martin laughed again. "Is that so? I didn't know that but I do know they are the most fascinating eyes I've ever seen!" He put out his hand to take hers and held it tightly.

They bumped for some minutes over rough gravel but soon the tires slid through soft grass and sand at the foot of the slope. Small cottages were dotted along the shore.

After a quick look around him Martin turned left into a lane and switched off the headlights. A pall of darkness closed around them and the empty houses, barely discernible against the night sky, stood bare-breasted and hostile like Zulus defending their own.

Martin put his arm protectively around Anthea. "Come on," he said, urging her out of the car. "I'll take you down first and then come back for our supper."

But she hung back. "I do wish we had a light," she whispered.

"So do I but we'll soon get used to the darkness," he said firmly. "It will be lighter on the sand and we're almost there."

Hesitantly Anthea stumbled forward in her high-heeled shoes, then stooped to remove them. Martin cursed silently. He should have realized that the cottages here were used only during the summer holidays and at the week-ends. It had not occurred to him that it would be unlit along this stretch of beach, and there was not even a flashlight in the car!

Some moments later they were on the beach, and Martin's feet grew heavy with the weight of silky dry sand pouring into his shoes with each step. As their eyes became accustomed to the gloom they stopped to look around them. The cove was deserted. Tiny waves rolled in and broke lazily upon a silvery beach. Not a whisper of wind disturbed the stillness but the air was cool. Martin could feel his heart thumping against his ribs.

"I've been dreaming of this moment," he murmured softly, tightening his arm around Anthea. "Here we shall be quite alone for once — just the two of us — and we have such a short time to be together."

Anthea turned towards him and rested her head against his chest. She smelled fragrant and he ached for love of her. He felt her trembling.

"What is it?" he asked gently. "Surely you can't be so cold!"

"Yes, I am cold, but I'm upset too. All day my mind has been going around and around in circles, spinning me out of control. I had the strangest feeling that I must hang on to something — anything — or I'd be whirled into some hellish pit. Then tonight . . . "

She stopped as if groping for words and Martin waited.

"Tonight . . . " she began again. "You won't ask me tonight, will you Martin? Not now. Not here. Promise me you won't do that?"

Martin felt as though a cold cloth had wrapped itself around him. He stiffened.

"Not if you don't want me to," he answered dully, his lips brushing against her hair, "but I thought you loved me."

"I do! Believe me, I do! But I didn't take my pills. Well — it's more than that! I've worked hard to get where I am. I just can't let a few rash moments destroy everything. And I won't. I WON'T!"

Martin was at a loss. He stroked her hair abstractedly.

"Darling, you know there are other ways . . ."

"No, no! Don't you see? I don't want you like this!"

Martin's arms slid slowly to his sides and hung limply down. He felt drained of emotion.

"All right — if that's how you feel. I'll take you home."

The words dropped from his lips without expression. Anthea did not want him! He didn't understand. He could not even begin to understand what had happened to her. She had behaved strangely all evening. Without a doubt he would find the cause in due course, but there was now so little time. Mechanically he helped her back across the sand and into the car, then slid behind the wheel.

As they headed homeward dejection

seemed to press down on him, numbing his limbs, dulling his mind. He kept repeating her words to himself, those words that had rocked his world: 'I don't want you like this.' Martin knew that the question was, 'Does she want me at all?' He was scarcely conscious of their ascent up the winding pathway to the main road, but a screeching of car tires ahead jolted him into awareness. Anger rose in a wave, almost choking him. He felt his heart beating faster.

Why the little b . . . ! She's been playing a game with me!

He stepped hard on the accelerator. The Mercedes leaped forward on the straight, screamed around a bend and then another, the headlights giving scant warning. Martin was beyond caring.

"After all I've planned!" he muttered under his breath. He had a wild impulse to end everything — there and then! Why not?

They were near to where his parents were killed, and he found himself wondering again, like a recurrent nightmare, about them. Had their end been quick or had those last few moments seemed an eternity? It would be so easy to turn the wheel a little too far, to step on the gas pedal instead of the brake. He and Anthea would die together, go hurtling over the huge rocks into the icy darkness of the sea! Perhaps they would be flung out in the downward plunge and sprawl lifeless on the flat-topped boulders, their faces smashed beyond recognition. A frightening picture flashed into his mind and he shuddered. No. He couldn't do this — not to Anthea!

"I'm sorry!" Her voice was low.

Martin continued to watch the road as if he had not heard but his foot eased its pressure. Presently he glanced over at Anthea.

"I don't understand you," he said. "We've seen a lot of each other these last few weeks and you know only too well how much I want you. You led me to believe you were not averse to the idea of a little lovemaking but now, suddenly, you don't want me! What have I done?"

"Don't be angry, please," she whispered. "Making love in those sorts of places fills me with revulsion, that's all."

"But, Anthea, if you loved me you would not care where we were."

She toyed with the scarf lying on her lap, twisting the corners into little knots, then spoke softly, eyes downcast.

"I know now I want the real thing, with God's blessing."

"Good Lord!" Martin exploded. "This is not 1820! And we are not children!"

Anthea continued to twist the corners of her scarf. "I can't help how I feel."

She put out her hand and rested it on his knee but he pushed it angrily away.

"Let me get this straight," he said, the words cracking like dry twigs. "You say you love me, but I'm not to be allowed to make love to you. Is that right?"

Anthea did no reply.

"You can't love me very much, can you?" His tone was drenched with sarcasm.

"Oh, Martin, dearest! How many times must I tell you? I love you more than anyone in the whole world, but that does not mean I'm going to let you turn our love into some distasteful affair."

"I see."

There was silence for a moment, then

Martin continued.

"And if my marriage breaks up or if something happens to give me my freedom, will you marry me then?"

"Of course, if I'm not married by that time."

"What do you mean by that?"

The car jerked as his foot slammed on the brake. Anthea shot forward in her seat but she did not explain.

Martin drew the Mercedes to the side of the road and stopped in a viewing point overlooking the Atlantic.

"I don't understand," he said, fighting to keep his voice controlled. "What do you mean — 'if I'm not married by that time?'"

Anthea lowered her eyes. "It's just that I might get married. I'd like a few children one day. You know that! I'm not getting any younger!"

"Yes, of course! I thought for the moment that you actually had marriage in mind."

"Well — that's right. I have."

Martin whistled softly through his teeth in disbelief.

"Are you serious?"

"Yes. Deadly serious! I didn't want to tell you, but now I've no choice. I'm thinking of getting married in July."

"You're thinking of WHAT?"

Anthea continued, her voice almost inaudible.

"You didn't ask me why I was late tonight and I didn't tell you. I was upset. I had a phone call from London. It was from someone I met when I was in England before Christmas. He's been writing to me since I left. I didn't think he was serious, but he is. He is arriving the first week in July and sailing on to Australia. He wants me to marry him while the ship is in dock here and go with him to Sydney."

Martin's heart was pounding so hard that he could scarcely speak.

"And what did you say?"

"I said I'd have to think it over."

"But you have just told me you love ME!"

"Martin, I do! Oh, sweetheart, I always will I suppose, but we'll have to stop seeing each other soon. There's no place for me in your life, not while there is Flora. But Michael is free!"

Goose pimples began to prickle as Martin broke out in a cold rash.

"My God!" he whispered. "You don't mean to tell me you've been quietly making your wedding plans while we've been going out these last few weeks?"

"Of course not! I told you! Michael phoned me tonight. I'll have to consider marrying him. It will be a way out for me — for us. I'd be a fool to turn him down. I could help him in his work and he'd help me in mine. We should probably make a great team. You can't expect me to stay here and torture myself day after day — to be near to you yet not with you! I'd go mad!"

As she spoke it seemed to Martin that her voice was far away, coming closer and closer in waves. What she said was indistinct but the meaning was clear. She was getting married — she was getting married — she was getting married! The words beat in his brain like a scratched phonograph record.

Suddenly his mind cleared. He had made his plans. He would see that they were carried out. It was as simple as that! It was not too late — he had until July.

"Let's talk about this some other time, shall we!" he said. Then with a studied calm he put the car back on the road and in silence they drove the rest of the way to Green point to Anthea's parked car, their picnic supper untouched on the seat behind them.

11

FLORA stood at the window in Beth's home in Edmonton trying to imprint the picture on her memory. She wished she could tuck it tenderly into a corner of her consciousness, to be rolled around and savoured slowly, like a sip of liqueur around the tongue, for this was to be her last visit. She knew it, just as she knew that twenty-four hours make each day. A feeling of fatality had hung like a shawl upon her shoulders ever since her arrival in Canada over three weeks ago. There seemed no way of shaking it off.

Wet snow had fallen during the night, and the boughs of spruce at the bottom of the garden drooped like bowed angels' wings over the ground. In the distance the river valley seemed to slumber peacefully under its coverlet of downy whiteness. The beauty moved Flora to sudden tears.

"To think I'll never see this again!" she murmured.

"Isn't it gorgeous?"

Flora swung around. Beth, framed in the doorway, held the baby in her outstretched arms. Flora nodded, took him into her arms and buried her face in the soft talcum-scented bundle as she struggled for composure.

"I didn't hear you come in," she said at last. "These shag carpets are luxurious, aren't they?" But her daughter was not to be side-tracked.

"Mother!" Beth said reprovingly, guiding Flora to the rocking chair and sitting down near her on the settee. "This is the second time today I've found you in tears! Whatever is it? You are on holiday, remember? And you've a brand new grandson just waiting to be loved and spoiled. Please try to snap out of whatever it is, at least before Arthur gets home!"

"I'm sorry!" Flora sniffed. "I've so much to be grateful for really, I don't know what gets into me."

She dabbed at her eyes with the corner of the baby's blanket, leaving a brown smudge and Beth snapped irritably, "Really, Mother! You have not changed one bit! Never a handkerchief at the crucial moment and always crying about something!"

She held out a tissue and Flora's lips quivered as she nodded her thanks. Beth's expression softened. She leaned over and rested her hand on her mother's arm.

"And I haven't changed either!" she said, her voice low. "I'm sorry! I always was a bit of a swine to you and here I am being spiteful again. I suppose subconsciously I was trying to punish you for not loving me."

"Not loving you!"

Flora patted Beth's cheek gently.

"How could I possibly not love my only child and a lovely daughter at that? I was not able to show it perhaps, but I've always loved you, of course, more than you'll ever know. I still do, even though you almost break my heart at times."

"I suppose I do," Beth answered softly, "but I don't mean to hurt you. I must have been thoroughly spoiled, but I don't get my own way very often now. Arthur is seeing to that! I don't like it one bit but I know it is good for me!"

She leaned back and rested her arm along the back of the settee.

"There was always Dad to look after me, and a succession of Angelines or Saras too, but I wanted you. My friends had mothers who showered them with love, but you remained in the background, seemingly not caring about me. I resented that! At prizegivings and concerts it was always just Dad! Weren't you interested in me?"

Flora looked down at the fair infant in her lap, at the immaculate fingernails on the small fingers resting so gently in the palm of her hand and she sighed.

"Your father and I made a pact when we were first married," she said. "It was understood that when you were born he would have complete control, that I would not interfere in any way in your upbringing."

"You agreed to that?" Beth's tone was disbelieving.

"There was no choice."

"I don't understand. I was half yours. Why should Dad want to deprive you of taking equal responsibility?"

"It was an agreement, as I said, before you were born."

Beth's arm dropped to her side. She leaned forward and colour suffused her cheeks.

"I think I understand. I was illegitimate, you mean?"

Flora shifted uncomfortably.

"No," she said. "But you could have been." The words had slipped out.

For some moments they looked at each other, then Flora lowered her eyes. Had she said too much?

Beth laughed shortly.

"That sounds intriguing! I always suspected there was something strange in our family set-up, so it doesn't surprise me, but — tell me about it. Please!"

Flora knew her daughter was watching her carefully but she did not look up. She was considering whether or not she dare tell her a little of the personal hell she had lived in for years — the private hell, largely of her own making. She had never before felt close enough, but now she felt a great need to confide in Beth. Tomorrow would be too late — Martin would have arrived. She looked up.

"You were born well over ten months after we got married," she said slowly, "but there's a bit more to the story than that!"

She started to rock the baby abstractedly, searching for the right words, and then softly, as if to herself she began.

"The day I first arrived in Cape Town from England I was attacked by ruffians."

Beth gasped. "How dreadful! You never told me!"

Flora nodded. "I never talk about it. I don't even like to think about it, even now! I was absolutely terrified, but Dad and Uncle Tom came to my rescue and later took me under their wings. I don't know what I should have done without them. I'd been quite on my own and the job waiting for me had called for an experienced bookkeeper. I knew it was but a matter of days, or perhaps weeks, before they found out how very inexperienced I was and it was a bad time for me. Uncle Tom lost no time in fixing me up with an extra job, three evenings a week, near the University. I was able to save more towards my ticket to Australia, but it enabled me to keep in touch with them too as one or the other would drive me home late at night, understanding my fear of another attack. In the weekends, if possible, they would take time off from their studies and we'd speed through the countryside or down to the beach, Dad behind the wheel and Uncle Tom spread out on the other side, resting his arm along the back of the seat. I would sit between them in my fragile heaven!"

She threw back her head and laughed. "Oh! How I dreamed then!" Her lips quivered suddenly.

"Uncle Tom would twine tendrils of my hair around his fingers or hold one of my hands in his large, hairy one or tickle me, pretending to count my many freckles. I would laugh with him but my eyes never left your father. I wanted so much to get to know him, really know him, to strip away the cool veil of good manners, to touch him somehow. I'd have done anything for him but he froze me with his polite regard. I thought I'd go crazy! I was so much in love!"

She broke off, conscious that she was talking not to herself but to her daughter.

"And then?" Beth prompted.

Flora smiled, then continued self-consciously.

"When the Christmas holidays arrived Uncle Tom went home to Durban. I heard nothing from Dad. A week passed. I knew then that I meant nothing to him, but my mind refused to believe it. I was miserable! Then, quite by chance, I read in an old newspaper about a car that had crashed onto the rocks at Oudekraal. Two people were killed. Their names rose out of the page before me as I read."

She paused, then lowered her voice.

"Your father had lost his parents — both of them — together!"

Beth nodded. "Dad told me about that once."

"All I could think of was that he would be alone and I must go to him. When I found him he was hiding in his flat, hoping everyone would think he had gone away after the funeral. I bribed the janitor to let me in. Dad looked awful! His eyes were hollow and red-rimmed, his chin covered in stubble and his clothes crumpled as if he had slept in them. He had, of course! Can you imagine? He had been called to identify the bodies and the horror of it burned into his mind until he thought he'd go mad. He tried to tell me about it. The words came, one or two at a time, and I had to piece them together. Suddenly he began to shiver and did not seem able to stop. I couldn't stand it! Somehow I got him into bed and put an extra blanket over him, but it did not help. I climbed in beside him, holding him close, warming him with my body, and for hours we lay together, not speaking. Gradually the cold lessened, bringing a deep calm and warmth, and — for the first time — an awareness of me."

Flora dabbed at her eyes with the tissue that she had rolled into a tight ball and a sob caught in her throat.

"Later — and it seemed somehow the most natural thing — we made love. I never questioned it."

Her hands began to tremble and the baby whimpered almost as if he understood. Flora hugged him to her and they rocked backwards and forwards as though comforting each other. Then Flora continued.

"The weeks passed and no mention was made of marriage. I was terrified I might be pregnant. You see, my knowledge was almost nil on that subject. I had assumed that Dad would lead me straight to the altar like any story-book hero, but his thoughts were on distant horizons: overseas study, experience in other lands. He meant to reach the top of his profession, that was certain, but where did I fit in? I saw myself growing old and grey and withered, alone and unloved. I knew I could not bear to see him go. I lied. I told him I was pregnant. I felt sure he would marry me and I was right, but when he discovered that I'd fooled him, I knew it was all over between us. I tried every way I knew to make it up to him, but it was no use. He has never forgiven me."

The last few words were a whisper as Flora came to the end of her narrative. Beth rose and knelt beside her. Gently she touched the fingers that restlessly folded and unfolded a portion of the baby's blanket.

"Didn't he care that you loved him?" she asked.

"He didn't believe me. Why should he? He'd caught me out in one lie already! He was certain it was all part of a deep scheme to get my hands on your grandfather's wealth!"

Beth shook her head in disbelief.

"If only I had known!" she whispered. "I could have helped in some way. I suppose it is too late now?"

"Oh, yes! Much too late!"

"But why did you stay together? Surely there was some other life waiting for you — for him?"

Flora stood up as the baby started to cry fretfully.

"I hardly know any more," she said softly. "Maybe because by that time I really was pregnant. You were on the way, and then when you were born I couldn't bring myself to leave you. At the time it seemed for the best that Dad and I stay together, keep up appearances for your sake and his career too. People's ideas were very rigid in those days! But perhaps the real reason was simply that I had nowhere to go!"

"I can scarcely believe it," Beth said. "And when Dad arrives tomorrow? What then? Can you calmly occupy the same bedroom, sleep in the same double bed?"

Flora smiled feebly. "It probably will be a bit of a shock to Dad to be so close to me again. We've had our own rooms for a long time, as you know, but we'll manage. He will be anxious to keep up appearances, as usual, and as for me — it will be easier now."

Beth rose and kissed her mother on the cheek.

"I'd have done more than drown my sorrows," she said. "I'd have killed myself!"

They looked into each other's eyes.

"I thought of that too," Flora said softly, "but that needs a lot of courage. I am not sure I have enough."

Beth smiled understandingly.

"But why did Dad keep you around after I left home? There was no career to worry about that time. He could have given you an allowance, given you another home."

"I've asked myself that many times," Flora answered, "and I haven't come up with a satisfactory answer. I filled the role of housekeeper, unnecessary though it was really, but perhaps it was that Dad never wanted ties with another woman so it was convenient to be married, even if in name only. I used to worry about what would happen if he fell in love."

She broke off abruptly. She had forgotten for the moment about Anthea. Her heart started a staccato beating in her chest.

"I still do."

The words were barely audible and her hands had begun to shake again. Beth took the baby and helped her mother back into the rocking chair.

"Don't, Mother, please!" she implored. "You are just torturing yourself! It is not likely that after all these years Dad will want to be tied to anyone. In any case, why should he not talk it over sensibly with you? And he would always provide for you, if that is what's worrying you."

Flora nodded.

"Yes, I suppose he would," she agreed. "I get depressed sometimes and my imagination skips around. I'm such a fool!"

Beth rested a hand on her mother's shoulder. "Aren't we all? Everyone does foolish things from time to time. The important thing is not to do anything that hurts. You have never hurt anyone in your life, not even Dad. He only imagines you have! I wish I had been a bit more like you, had a real heart to motivate me!"

Flora looked up and smiled through the tears that had suddenly blurred her vision.

"That is the nicest thing you have ever said to me!"

Beth smiled back.

"There were many nice things I could have said and didn't! I'm sorry. I'll have to make it up to you somehow, but you'll have to be patient. I won't be able to change overnight, remember, but I can try!"

She tucked her head into the baby's soft neck and walked quickly out of the room. As she went Flora realized she too was crying. It occurred to her that it was the first time she had known her daughter to weep from emotion. She had cried for attention many times. This was something different. Her girl had grown up at last. She was a wife and a mother now. She understood.

* * *

That night Flora went up early to bed but not to sleep. Try as she would she could not relax, and for hours she tossed around in the wide double bed. Martin would arrive the following evening. Unless Beth changed her plans, he would be sharing this very bed with her! She had told Beth it would be easier now, but she had forgotten that Martin always read her thoughts. She might even talk in her sleep! It would be but a matter of moments before he learned about Jock. He would say nothing, of course, but he would know and she would know that he knew! Her head ached and she felt nauseated from tension. What would he do to her? What could he do?

Hoping for oblivion, she drank the remainder of the brandy in her flask, but it only made her feel sicker than ever and by the morning she was too ill to get out of bed.

Beth pottered anxiously around, bringing aspirins, cold cloths and antacids, but to no avail.

"Oh, Mother!" she said despairingly, "If only this had not happened today! Dad will never believe you've been so well up to now! Only a few hours and I'll have to meet him at the airport!"

"I'm sorry to be such a nuisance," Flora said, weakly lifting her hand to adjust a fresh cold cloth across her forehead. "It must have been that brandy. But I don't understand — there was only a little left. Please don't tell Arthur! He will be so disgusted with me!"

Beth frowned. "Really, Mother!" she said. "Arthur won't eat you alive, you know! But I've got the answer! I am going to hide your flask and lock up all the alcohol in the house until you get over this spell of nausea. What do you say to that?"

Flora looked up at her daughter and laughed feebly.

"Of course, my darling, if you like," she said. "I'm not an alcoholic, you know. I can stop any time I please. I don't HAVE to have a drink. I just

WANT to! Your father knows this too, otherwise why didn't he lock up the liquor cabinet at home?"

Beth looked thoughtful. "That's true," she said. "Nevertheless, I'm banning all alcohol in this house until you are well again." She looked at her mother and smiled again.

"I suppose actually you have been working yourself into a state about Dad coming home. Am I right?"

Flora smiled reluctantly.

"I suppose so. It is quite ridiculous! Dad and I have never been able to talk to each other — really talk as wives and husbands should — yet I keep hoping!" She shook her head impatiently. "Did you know that I used to collect all your old text books from school? I read them carefully, answered the set questions, struggled with French verbs, studied Ruskin and many others, read through masses of volumes from cover to cover — Dickens, Shakespeare, Voltaire and so on, just to improve my sketchy education and be able to hold my own in discussing interesting topics with Dad, and we never even discussed the weather!"

Beth's mouth had fallen open.

"I can't believe it!" she gasped.

"Yes," Flora continued, "it was all a gigantic waste of effort, and now Dad has someone he is interested in at the hospital. He denies it, but I know it is true and can't help worrying. Do you think she will want to marry him?"

Beth put her hand on her mother's and patted it reassuringly.

"Maybe — IF there is someone, as you say. But will Dad want to marry her? It won't do you any good to worry about it, and if marriage is what they want, won't that be a blessing? You would be free to find someone else."

Flora nodded, then closed her eyes as her daughter hurried downstairs. Beth made it all sound so simple but then she would never believe her father capable of anything as base as murder. Flora knew better and knew too that it would be no simple matter to pay with one's life, for — sooner or later — that was something she would have to do. She knew it because Martin had said she would have to and she had never known him to change his mind.

12

THE DC-8 seemed to be enveloped in flames as it chased the sun down to the horizon, but as it approached the airfield it dipped through low cloud into a world of grey. It levelled slowly off, bumped unsteadily onto the tarmac, then roared suddenly, as if in protest, and taxied at a brisk pace towards the terminal building.

Martin peered disinterestedly through the windows at the wet runway bounded by banks of melting snow. So this was Edmonton, he thought. A study in grey and white! It meant nothing. He might just as well have been in some remote part of Siberia. He shrugged. It didn't really matter. He had come for a purpose — not for a holiday as everyone supposed.

Flora must be given regular doses of two kinds of pills — enough to keep her nauseated and to establish, if possible, that she had a liver complaint. Both sets were to be administered after meals, with a little bicarbonate of soda, for at least one week. He knew that simultaneous administration would aggravate the toxicity of each drug. If she reacted as he hoped, all he would have to do would be to sit back and watch results. By the time Flora left by train en route to England, Beth should have accepted the fact that her mother was ill. That was all that he needed at present but he knew he would have to be careful. He must not overdo the drugs or Flora might not feel well enough to travel.

He unbuckled his seat belt and thankfully unwound his stiff legs from under him. It had been an arduous flight and he wished now he'd spent a day in Paris. He had not been able to sleep during the sixteen-hour night flight up Africa, in spite of having three seats to stretch out upon in the Boeing 707. Then, barely rested at Orly Airport, he'd had to face the second half of the trip to Canada. A full plane had meant constant noise and interruptions and he had managed to doze only once or twice the entire way. His head throbbed and his eyes seemed to roll on sand.

Now his Beth would be out there waiting, but he was almost too exhausted to care. He told himself he did not feel the same about her now, anyway, for he had never quite forgiven her for running away — and that really was what she had done — but he was not entirely convinced.

He remembered every detail of the day she left with Arthur. Confetti and rose petals had left a trail as she raced excitedly down the circular staircase and across the hall and there they had lain all through the night, as though in mourning: small crushed flowers upon an open grave. Next day all had been swept into a cold tidiness, and it seemed to Martin that part of him had been swept away too, never to return.

Automatically he reached for his raincoat and put it on with no interruption to his flow of thoughts.

Now that Beth was a wife and mother, would they be able to recapture their close harmony one with the other, or had that too been but a childish thing discarded with the old toys when she married Arthur?

With a sigh he buttoned his plaid-lined Burberry, turning the collar well up over his scarf, then, picking up his flight bag and hat, he stepped in line to deplane.

As he passed through the open glass doors countless faces were turned in his direction. He looked carefully around but the eyes showed no interest or recognition. There was no one here that he knew, and he'd flown over 9,500 miles to be with his family! He felt suddenly as flat as old ale. So Beth hadn't cared enough! All at once he knew that he cared — a great deal — about seeing her! It was no use fooling himself.

After waiting about dejectedly a few minutes, Martin followed an arrow that indicated 'Baggage' and stood pensively watching as suitcases and packages came tumbling onto the moving conveyer belt.

The next moment arms encircled him from behind and Beth's voice said huskily, "Dad! Oh, Dad! Is it really you?"

He turned and hugged her close to him, trembling with the nearness of her, then abruptly he held her at arm's length.

He noticed she wore slightly more make-up. Her fine, blonde hair had been swept neatly back and styled by expert fingers, her clothes were elegant and her figure a shade fuller around the bust line.

"Beth, my angel!" he said. "You've changed! I've lost my girl!"

His voice had sounded amazed yet delighted, and Martin sensed she was embarrassed.

She laughed up at him, not meeting his eyes.

"Yes. I'm very much an overweight, nursing mother right now," she said, "but I'm working on it! Just give me time!" and she kissed him lightly on the cheek.

"I'm so sorry I'm late, Dad," she went on, "but there was a bit of a scramble at home. Arthur had an important meeting tonight and I had to find a baby-sitter at the last moment."

"And Mother?"

Beth looked down. "She wasn't well enough to come, but we kept hoping she would be. You won't believe me, Dad, but Mom was wonderfully well at first. Then this morning she started being ill — the very day you were due to arrive!"

"Has she been drinking again do you think?"

Beth flushed and Martin remembered that she had always hated any mention of this hurtful topic.

"No. Just an occasional drink before dinner, I think, until last night. She may have overdone it a bit after she went up to bed. I noticed the flask was empty this morning."

"That's too bad!" Martin said, but what he felt was a great jubilation. This was going to be too easy!

"It's such a strain on her liver when she does that," he went on. "Has she seen a doctor?"

"No. I knew she wouldn't hear of it. She feels self-conscious — doesn't even want Arthur to know she drank that brandy! And then you were coming and would know better than anyone what to give her."

Martin leaned forward to remove his

suitcases from the rack. Flora was just asking for the special pills he had brought with him from South Africa! And this latest drinking bout? What was she trying to hide from him this time? It would be interesting to find out!

He looked around for a porter and Beth smiled.

"One of the first things we learn in Canada is that it is a do-it-yourself land, Dad! There are porters, but we carry our own bags here unless we are infirm or have large trunks. I'll give you a hand."

Martin hastily picked up the luggage.

"Of course," he said, waving her away. "It was thoughtless of me. I hadn't realized how spoiled we are in South Africa, with the millions of black hands anxious or willing to help for a coin."

"And without a coin, too," his daughter admonished. "Be fair, Dad!"

"Yes, you are right," he added looking around him. "Maybe I am being unfair."

So Beth was thinking for herself these days, he thought sadly. There had been a time when she would not have questioned anything he said.

"I don't see any dark faces here," he remarked, to take his mind off his sudden disturbing thoughts.

"Perhaps not at this moment, but there are more than one would think — visitors and students from all parts of the world, all colours, races, and creeds. Many applied for citizenship while here and their cases were speeded up to allow them to remain, but a new immigration policy has changed that. Application now has to be made from outside Canada so the influx will be slower, I suppose. The majority will still return, I'm sure. It's a good land. There's no oppression here, a good minimum wage and — as they say — 'equal opportunity for all.' We've been told we need immigrants but employment has never been such a problem and they have to be careful."

She opened the trunk of the car and looked up at her father as he placed his bags neatly inside.

"I'm glad I came, Dad. I miss the beaches and the magnificent Cape scenery, of course, but this is my home now and I love it. I feel safe and my life is spent more creatively. I had not realized how much time I wasted playing tennis, swimming and hiking — in fact just having a glorious loaf in the sun! I'm probably in tip-top condition because of it, but I'm using my brain more here. The long evenings in winter encourage one to read. When Jamie is a bit older I intend to return to night school to brush up on my English. I may even go back to the University and finish that B.A. I started."

Martin patted her fondly on the arm.

"I'm so glad, my darling," he said. "Learning is one way to keep from being lonely and with books one can always escape from the unpleasant or the humdrum. Unfortunately one can get tired of learning. I've suddenly got fearfully bored with medical textbooks. I'm relieved to be able to relax and enjoy myself for a change."

He yawned and Beth hastily opened the car door and climbed in, stretching across to open the door for her father.

"We'd better get home," she said. "Mother will be anxious to see you."

Martin smiled inwardly. 'Anxious' was probably not the correct word. If he were any judge of women, Flora's attitude would be one of fear!

"I'm putting you in baby's room," Beth continued. "I thought you'd be tired and need your sleep. Jamie will be with us and Mother is in the guest room, of course."

"That's thoughtful of you, my dear," Martin said. "I admit I'll be glad of a good rest tonight, but in the morning I'll move in with Mother. The baby may keep Arthur awake and I should be with Mother, especially now that she's not well."

"All right, Dad, if that's what you think best."

Martin frowned. He wanted to keep an eye on Flora to make sure she took her pills but he could not very well explain this to his daughter.

"I can't believe I'm here at last!" he said, changing the subject abruptly. "I left Paris just after midday, spent thirteen hours flying and wasted roughly two hours with stops in Montreal and Toronto, yet it's only just after eight o'clock! It's been almost like sitting in a stationary plane today while they moved boards of sky scenery past windows, as in the old movies. I seemed to be making no headway and living the minutes over and over."

He yawned again and Beth smiled at him.

"You must be exhausted, Dad, but we'll soon be home. You can have a glorious hot bath and sleep the clock around. When you finally wake you'll see the sun shining brightly and you'll know it was worth coming! Everything will soon be a lovely fresh green under that wet snow, and it's melting fast. The buds are stirring with new life. You can almost hear them! In a few days we'll realize that spring is here with its colourful crocuses and silky pussy willows. You'll love it!"

She kept talking brightly, and as Martin listened he realized she was shy of him now. There was a small undercurrent of restraint and for a while he could not pinpoint why. Suddenly he knew, just as he had always known what was in her mind. She was telling him that she loved him and always would but that she was married now and belonged to Arthur.

Martin placed his hand over hers on

the steering wheel.

"Dearest Beth," he whispered.

She gripped his fingers tightly, then lifted them to her cheek and held them there. Martin felt a tear drop onto the back of his hand.

★ ★ ★

Meanwhile, in Beth's beautiful house in Edmonton, Flora gathered her battery of cosmetics around her. Martin must not see her like this, she thought, desperation giving her shaking hands a semblance of skill. He had always hated to see her ill, and she knew she looked ghastly with her pale face and dark halfmoons under her eyes. She was dreading the meeting with him — dreading his searching into her soul. She couldn't face hatred as well, not yet!

She brushed her hair and applied foundation cream, liquid make-up, and rouge, but she was not satisfied. She dabbed spots of glue on her new false eyelashes and fixed them shakily in place. They were not perfectly straight but she told herself she could keep the light dim. Feeling miraculously better for the moment, she climbed back into bed, but the empty place beside her haunted her. She knew Beth had arranged for Martin to sleep in the baby's room that night and she was determined that arrangement — or a similar one — should stand, for she had worked herself into near hysteria visualizing the interminable nights ahead with both she and Martin stiff as corpses for fear of one inadvertently touching the other, and what was even worse, imagining new horrors because of her fear that he meant to get rid of her while they were away from home. How would she know when he might decide to place a pillow over her face and press down, relentlessly? And what if it was his intention to poison her?

Eventually, a cool sanity had returned. Flora felt reasonably sure that Martin would not attempt anything while living with Beth. He would want to spare his darling, of course! Flora began to relax and by the time she heard the car drive up to the house, she was in good control of herself and ready to play the little family game of 'Let's Pretend.'

13

AFTER Martin's arrival Flora seemed a jangle of nerves, her stomach unable to tolerate the lightest meal. As she had expected, Martin produced pills for her to take and she was quick to notice they were different from those he had given her in South Africa. She had presumed the previous pills to be a type of tranquilizer and an anti-emetic, for one had calmed her and eventually induced sleep, while the other had cured her nausea and vomiting. The new pills alarmed her. She was tempted not to take them but with Beth near she felt safe enough and decided it would be better to see what effect they had on her. After all, she thought, they might be only an improvement on the old medication or due to the fact that Canadian drugs were different in appearance yet contain the same ingredients. But after several days on the new pills she felt no better and determined to obtain a couple for analysis. She wanted to know why they were being given to her if they were not curing her symptoms and were not poison.

An opportunity presented itself sooner than she had dared to hope. After dinner one evening Martin handed Flora her pills and a small medicine glass of bicarbonate of soda, as Beth brought the baby into the room. Martin's attention was momentarily diverted and Flora wasted no time. Quickly she dropped the pills inside her nightgown and drank the liquid in the usual way. It had been a simple manoeuvre and she had her precious pair, later wrapping them carefully and hiding them in her handbag until such time as she could get to a druggist.

Some days later Flora noticed that her skin was tinged a dark shade of yellowish orange. She turned this way and that in front of the bathroom mirror, but there was no doubt about it. Slowly she crept back to her bedroom and sank down heavily on the edge of the bed, her mind incapable of thought. It seemed to spin in circles and then congeal into a ball of lard. She stared in front of her.

"Another lovely day!"

Beth's cheery voice startled Flora but she managed to smile. "Yes," she answered mechanically. "Isn't it?"

Setting down the morning tea tray, Beth helped her mother into bed. "I thought we might give Jamie his first outing in the new pram this afternoon," she went on. "How do you feel?"

"Much the same really," Flora answered. "Up and down like a see-saw but at the moment I feel more tired than ill. Maybe I'll enjoy a walk later on, as long as it isn't too far." She looked up at her daughter waiting for some comment on her colour, but none came.

"Good!" Beth clipped, opening the curtains a little wider. "Arthur has invited Dad to lunch at the Club, so we can have ours early and stroll along in the sunshine toward the zoo. Jamie might even get some roses in his cheeks — and you too!"

With that she bustled out again without specific mention of having noticed any change in her mother, yet moments later, as she reached the foot of the stairs, Flora heard her say, "Dad, do you think Mother looks a bit jaundiced this morning, or is it my imagination?"

Obviously Beth had not realized that voices would carry so audibly up the stairway. Flora lay absolutely still and listened while her heart seemed to bang like a gong inside her.

"I hadn't noticed," Martin answered, "but I'll take a look when I go in after breakfast. Don't say anything yet, will you? It will only upset Mother and we don't want to worry her unduly, but remember we do have to expect certain symptoms with her liver in its present condition."

Flora's mouth opened in astonishment. First Tom and now Martin, she thought. What was all this about her liver? Was something wrong? Then why had she not been told and why hadn't someone been consulted? She had not had a medical examination in years! She leaned back weakly on the pillows and stared unseeingly at the ceiling.

Maybe Martin was not planning to murder her after all. She was going to die from a diseased liver — if that was what it was. Suddenly she was furiously angry. Why should she sit quietly by while Martin allowed her to slip into the grave like this for his own dim purposes? Maybe there was a cure for her. She had a right to know what was happening. Her lips trembled as vexation and fear struggled for supremacy, then she closed her eyes and gave way to tears.

The next instant she was conscious of a light step on the carpet and realized that someone was standing silently beside her bed. Her heart gave a sudden flutter. So Martin had not finished his breakfast after all! She opened her eyes and looked straight into his. The unguarded expression she saw there made her catch her breath. The tears froze on her face. She continued to look at him and then slowly shook her head in disbelief.

"Oh, my God!" she whispered. "You are actually glad I'm ill. GLAD! Why — you're inhuman, MAD!" Her voice had risen. She struggled to sit up. Martin hastily closed the door behind him and held his fingers to his lips.

"For goodness sake don't make a scene!" he hissed, keeping his voice low.

"Arthur is downstairs! I don't know what has got into you this time, but please try to control yourself for Beth's sake. We don't want our visit to turn into a disaster!"

Flora lay back again in the pillow. Martin was right, as usual. It was unfair to bring their problems to Beth's home. They had not even been invited! Martin had merely written to say they were coming for a visit. Arthur probably had not been too happy about it, but he had been kind enough to welcome them. It was up to them not to make things difficult during their stay.

Silently she motioned with her hand for Martin to leave her. When he had closed the door again she turned over and buried her face in the cool pillow. Outside she heard Martin say, "I think you are right. Your mother does look a bit jaundiced. We must just watch it awhile and see it gets no worse," and then the warm air conditioner commenced to whir and the rest was lost to her.

★ ★ ★

It was some while before Flora managed to dress, but with great determination this was at last accomplished. By the time she went down to her lunch of dry crackers and bouillon her mind seemed to be working again. She could scarcely keep up with all the ideas that popped up and then burst like bubbles in a boiling sauce.

There were several things she would have to do, she told herself. She must try to be orderly and attend to them one by one, but first of all she would have to get some strength. There were three days left before she was due to leave by train for Halifax, there to board her ship for England, where Martin was to meet her. She must be well enough to leave as scheduled or Martin might force her to fly with him to England.

Slowly she crumbled a cracker into the bowl and started to eat. One thing was certain. She must get away from Martin to have a complete physical checkup as soon as possible. Only then could she begin to pick up the pieces in her shattered world. Her mouth twisted grimly. She had been prepared to feign illness to keep Martin from her room and all the while Old Man Death was stealing up behind her in slippered feet!

Suddenly all fear seemed to drain away leaving a sediment of calm to sooth her.

"After all, what is death?" she asked herself. "Can it be so much worse than a living hell?"

14

THE loudspeaker crackled above the noise of talking and laughter and a voice said "Super Continental Train No. 2 is now arriving from Vancouver . . . "

"Well — this is it!" Beth said hugging Flora close to her. "I do wish you had not insisted on leaving today. Another week would have helped you get on your feet." She kissed her mother on a still yellow cheek. "Take good care of yourself and please telephone from Halifax. I'll be so anxious!"

"I will, dear. And thank you for everything. Look after the wee one! I shall miss him!"

Martin raised an eyebrow in amusement. Quite a touching family scene, he said to himself, his lower lip curling arrogantly. He'd never before noticed any marked affection one for the other, but he supposed distance had lent enchantment! Well — it was his turn now to put on a show! He stepped forward.

"Now, you have everything?" he asked. "Tickets, passport, travellers' cheques?"

Flora nodded.

"Good."

He bent over and gave her the usual cold, dutiful peck on the side of her cheek. Their eyes met.

"Don't forget to confirm the sailing time as soon as you reach Halifax," he said. "The ship should be in port and you'll be able to go straight on board. If not, for some reason, go to the hotel as arranged."

Flora nodded again.

"I'll be in Southampton to meet you," Martin continued, "but if I'm delayed you know what to do — take a taxi over to the *S.S. Glenconnor* and wait for me there. I've written the name on the cover of your travellers' cheques in case you forget it. Now — you had better hurry!"

Flora blew a kiss to Beth and turned to join the queue moving at a steady pace through the glass doors leading to the railway platform. She walked carefully, with back slightly bent. As she reached the steps she looked back without smiling and waved, then swung left and moved forward out of sight.

For a moment Beth and Martin stared after her, then they turned away and walked silently through the crowd, up the escalator to the exit leading to the car park.

As Beth settled herself behind the wheel of her Jaguar, she blew her nose vigorously into her handkerchief, and Martin was amazed to realize that she genuinely had been upset at leaving her mother. He did not like it! Beth had always been his girl. Had Flora usurped his position? He should not have left them alone, he told himself. He should have known that Flora would sneak her way somehow into Beth's heart. And what had she been telling the girl?

Beth drove the short distance down 101st Street and across Jasper Avenue in silence, then she said, "It's a bit early, but I'm going to take you to tea at the top of the Chateau Lacombe. There is a revolving restaurant up there and one can see for miles around. It is something I've been saving for us. We can relax and talk with no baby to disturb us and no invalid trays to worry about either."

Martin looked across at her.

"I'm sorry that you have had all this running around with Mother ill," he said. "I should not have brought her really, but it did not seem fair not to let her see the baby."

Beth sighed.

"I did not mean it that way," she said. "I'm only too glad that Mother took ill where I was able to look after her, and I enjoyed showing her a little love for a change. It was long overdue! I'm just a bit exhausted, that's all!"

She drove into the hotel car park and climbed out quickly, banging the door after her.

"I'm so depressed, too!" she went on. "Four weeks ago Mother walked in through those same glass doors she went out of today. I wish you could have seen her then. She came tripping along, full of smiles and obviously well. I just can't believe the change in her! It is staggering! This is what I want to talk to you about."

She led the way unhesitatingly into the

hotel, straight across the lobby and into the elevator. Martin followed silently. He recognized she was in one of her moods. He would have to tread warily. When they were seated and had ordered their tea, he reached across the small table and patted Beth's hand reassuringly.

"Don't worry so much, darling," he said. "Mother has been abusing her liver for years! This reaction is exactly what I had expected, especially after the long voyage without my eagle eye upon her!"

Beth looked crossly at him, her chin jutting forward in a gesture of disapproval.

"But, Dad!" she said. "I've told you! She came off that train looking better than I'd seen her in years. She had a few small drinks with us at home and only one possible 'session' as you call it, and that the night before your arrival. I can't believe it was that! I was wondering whether these attacks could be psychological — brought on to gain attention or perhaps through fear?"

Martin sat back in his chair as the tea was placed before them, and glanced quickly away. He placed his hands carefully together, stretching his fingers in pairs to form a steeple.

"I'm no expert in that field," he said at last, choosing his words with care, "but I should imagine anything is possible. I don't believe, however, that the nausea is psychological and certainly not the jaundice — not in your mother's case. She isn't looking for attention from me and has no reason to fear me that I can see!"

His eyes challenged Beth's. She lowered her eyes and Martin continued.

"The unhappy truth is that she has lived a life of indolence and has always indulged herself. Now it is beginning to show, that is all!"

There was silence as Beth poured the tea and handed a cup to her father. Martin took a few sips, then placed the cup slowly in the saucer.

"What to do about Mother's condition is the real problem, though, not the reason for it."

"I don't agree!" said Beth shortly. "If you would bother to get to the root of the trouble — why she drinks — she would perhaps not drink so much. As a result she wouldn't be damaging her liver. It's simple, isn't it?"

Her lips had curled disdainfully and Martin felt his heart beginning to pound inside his chest. It was almost as if he were looking at himself in female form! Was she actually disagreeing with him, trying to put him in his place? He couldn't believe it! The muscles in his cheek twitched with anger.

"Don't you realize it's too late for that?" he hissed, leaning forward in his chair and looking straight at her again. "I didn't think I'd have to spell it out! I thought you'd understand."

Beth put her hand to her mouth and stared wide-eyed at him.

"Why do you think I brought her all this way?" he went on. "To visit you and her grandchild before it's too late! Surely you realized?"

Beth shook her head slowly.

"But why was she so well at first?"

"These things happen — don't ask me why! But they can't last and when the final plunge starts it is fantastically quick. You'll have to face facts, my darling.

Your mother doesn't have much time. This is terminal!"

Beth's lips quivered.

"It can't be!" she said softly. "I can't believe it!"

Martin sat back in his chair and waited for his words to penetrate.

Finally Beth spoke.

"Does she know?"

"I haven't actually told her," Martin answered, "but I know she suspects."

"What are you going to do?"

"There isn't much anyone can do really, but when we get home she will have to go into Groote Schuur for treatment. She has lost a lot of weight and of course the jaundice is a bad sign."

Beth nodded.

"Poor Mother! No wonder she was so terribly depressed. To think I was irritable about it too! Oh — I'm a beast!"

She began to cry softly. Martin took her hands in his.

"My dearest, don't let it upset you so much," he said. "We all have to go some time. And she's had a very easy life

— not lifted a finger, never been short of a thing!"

Beth pulled her hands away and brushed the tears impatiently from her eyes.

"Maybe no material things!" she snapped, "but we certainly didn't bend over backwards to see she had any love or affection, did we?"

They glared at each other, then Beth continued.

"It must have been sheer hell for her living with us. I should have understood. You enjoyed being cruel to her, depriving her of everything that matters in this world, and I took my cue from you always — like a bit of you, broken off, living and breathing alone, but a part of you still! I'm not proud of my role in this!"

She turned away and stared out of the window at the panorama spread beneath her. The swollen river swirled sullenly through the valley, its patches of ice bobbing and twirling southward. The earth, a dark brown carpet, spread as far as the eye could see, was splashed with white where the sun's warmth had not yet reached. Upon it in orderly rows lay the houses like tiny red and green children's blocks.

"I love you so much, Dad," she said, "but I wish I hadn't believed so implicitly in you. I'm only now realizing! You are not always right! How am I to be certain you are right now about Mother! Have you consulted anyone about her?"

Martin shook his head.

"I never thought the day would come when my vast medical knowledge would be questioned by a young whippersnapper," he said. He was smiling but the smile had not reached his eyes. Deeply angry he was holding tightly to his control. Beth had to be convinced, not shouted at. She was looking steadily at him.

"You haven't answered my question," she said quietly, picking up her cup of tea and taking a sip.

Martin glowered at her, then put back his head and laughed.

"You're my girl!" he joked, "but you don't yet know your father! Of course I haven't 'consulted anyone,' as you put it. Do you think I want everyone in town to know the unpleasant details about my alcoholic wife?"

"But she isn't an alcoholic — not a true one! If she were, would you keep any alcohol in the house? Or did you perhaps want her to drink to destroy herself?"

"This is a nightmare!" Martin exploded. "I can't believe it! My own daughter hurling accusations at me!"

Beth set down her cup.

"Dad!" she said softly. "Since you arrived I've kept having the most horrible nightmares. I told myself they were just bad dreams but now I'm more disturbed than ever. I'm so afraid they are real after all! You haven't really answered my questions, you've evaded them!"

She put her hands up to her face as sobs suddenly shook her body.

Martin stared at her.

"What do you want me to say?" he asked, his voice low. "That your mother isn't an alcoholic in the true sense? Maybe she isn't but who cares? Whenever she had anything to hide from me, she drank. I had to stand by and watch it. Does it matter that she is not a true alcoholic? I could have been a great man if it hadn't been for her — and not only in medicine! I wanted to be a politician — a figure of some consequence to my country, but no! I had to skulk in a back alley because of my wife. I didn't dare attend any function with her in case she disgraced me. She knew right from the start that she had failed me, but she clung to me — to all the material things I had to offer."

He leaned across the table again.

"I didn't need to wish she would destroy herself," he hissed. "She set about doing that quite on her own and very methodically many years ago! The miracle is that she didn't drag me down with her. What did you expect me to do? What would you have done if you'd been in my shoes? Answer me!"

Beth's shoulders continued to heave with her silent sobs. She shook her head.

"Oh, God! I don't know," she whispered. "I don't know anything anymore! I was my father's daughter. I thought I knew exactly who I was and where I was going. Now I find I'm just playing second fiddle to Arthur's ambition! Did you realize that? I'm fighting for my place in the sun! How can I possibly help my mother? How can I help you? If it were not for my baby I'd be lost! He's all I have now and he doesn't even know it!"

Tears poured down her face and she began to laugh hysterically. Then she rose and pushed back her chair.

"Let's go home," she said, and picking up her bag and gloves she swept toward the exit.

Martin fumbled for his wallet as the waitress' curious eyes followed Beth's retreating figure.

"Could I please have the bill?" he asked quietly and then — his air of nonchalance momentarily returning to save the day — he sauntered after her.

15

THE sleek Trans Continental glided slowly into Halifax Station and hissed aggressively to a standstill alongside the platform. Flora climbed shakily down, taking in great gulps of none-too-fresh air as though it were ozone. It was a relief to be on firm ground again for the trip from Edmonton had been an endurance test, the nausea seemingly aggravated by the motion of the train.

She felt a great need to rest in a quiet hotel, or even the freighter, if she had docked, but first of all she must find a druggist. For her peace of mind it was imperative for her to discover the contents of the pills she had wrapped so carefully in Edmonton and secreted in her handbag. When she had finished the business of storing her bags and with the receipts safely tucked away in one of the many recesses of her large handbag, she set off to the nearest coffee shop.

After a cup of clear tea and a beef sandwich she felt strong again, and anxious to move on. She telephoned from the call-box in the coffee shop and learned that the freighter was due to dock early the following morning. She wasted no time. As she paid her bill she asked the cashier about nearby drugstores and quiet hotels and was given explicit directions. She decided to walk and before long she was standing before a store that looked fairly large and clean. Inside were several young women assistants, but they did not fit the picture in her mind. She was about to turn away when, behind the prescription counter she noticed an elderly bald man with pince-nez about to fly off the tip of his nose. He had a sweet expression and a lovely smile. Flora walked over and stood waiting as he served a customer.

"May I help you, Madam?" he said at last.

"I hope so," she answered smiling. "I have a couple of pills with me. Will it be possible for you tell me what they contain?"

He took a hard look at her. "Were they

prescribed for you?" he asked.

"Yes, but not by a Canadian doctor."

"I see. And you are taking them now?"

"I had been."

"You were not well?"

"That is right. But I was not told what was wrong with me. I am hoping to get some idea when I know what the pills are and what they were prescribed for."

"The doctor did not tell you then?"

"No."

The man hesitated a moment and then he held out his hand.

"I'll see what can be done."

Shakily Flora removed the small wad of tissue paper from an inside pocket of her handbag and handed it over. He unwrapped the pills carefully and glanced down at them, then he picked up a magnifying glass and scrutinized them closely under a bright light. As he put them down on the counter he looked across at Flora.

"May I please have your name and address?" he asked, drawing a notebook and pen his way.

Flora hesitated. She did not want

Martin to know about this, at least until after she had seen the report.

"Is my name absolutely necessary?" she asked and the druggist flashed a quick smile at her.

"I'm afraid so, Madam. You see, these pills may not have been made in Canada. It could take a little while . . . " he shrugged his shoulders apologetically.

Flora nodded understandingly. Had Martin brought them all the way from South Africa? But why?

"How long do you think it will take?" she asked.

"Maybe a week or even more, but it really depends on how busy they are at the lab."

"Oh, but I have to sail in a day or so," she said, disappointment washing through her. "Can you hurry them up do you think?"

"I can try, but they are usually a few days behind and the weekend will be coming up again. The days seem to have gone that working overtime to help customers was the rule. I'm sorry!"

Flora leaned heavily on the counter. There seemed to be no point in trying elsewhere for speedier service, for that might mean fruitless walking around and she felt almost too tired to drag one weary foot after the other.

"Would it be too much trouble for you to call the lab now? If I know for sure they will only have the results after I sail, then perhaps you can telegraph them to me on the ship or to my home in South Africa."

"South Africa, Madam? Oh, certainly."

With a curious look at her over the top of his pince-nez, the old gentleman walked behind the glass screen. When he returned a few minutes later Flora saw by the look on his face that he had had no luck.

"I really am sorry," he said, pursing his lips and shaking his head slowly. "The end of next week at the earliest! But leave me your name and that of the ship to South Africa. I shall see that the results are sent immediately they are available."

"Thank you," Flora said, "but please make sure they are sent to me personally on board the *S.S. Glenconnor*. She is sailing from Southampton and due to dock in Cape Town on the 15th of June."

"Certainly! And Bon Voyage."

"Thank you."

Flora did not like this arrangement but there seemed little else that she could do. If the results were telegraphed to the ship they might fall into Martin's hands, but she would have to take a chance. Perhaps she could mention the grave importance of the matter to the Purser when Martin was not around.

Carefully she wrote the details asked and paid the fee. While waiting for her change she noticed a rack of notebooks and diaries on the counter. One in particular interested her. The words *Diary of my Trip* were embossed in gold lettering on a red leather cover. On a sudden impulse she took it from the rack and turned it over in her hands.

During her stay with Beth she had taken to jotting down on scrap paper little items of interest — the day the baby first smiled up at her, the day snow fell as if for her benefit, the day Martin spoke to Beth without knowing that she had heard their voices up the stairway.

She had found it a great comfort to write down her thoughts. It was as if she had at last found a friend who understood, a friend who thought as she did. All her ideas, all her dreams and fears, were jotted down, at first hesitantly as if she found it difficult to express herself after so long a silence, but later fluently, the words chasing each other across the pages now that the rust in her creaking mind was rubbed smooth by constant use.

"I'd like this, please," she said, holding out the diary and once more handing over several dollars and some coins. "You don't need to wrap it. It will fit in my bag."

Then, having completed for the time being the business she had earmarked 'Priority No. 1' in her plan of action, she set off slowly to find the nearest quiet-looking hotel. She would enjoy one more night on dry land before embarking. She had packed a nightdress, toothbrush and a change of underwear in her roomy handbag for she had discovered that bags could be a nuisance when travelling alone. In the morning, if she felt well enough, she might take a scenic tour around the city before collecting her belongings and boarding the freighter to England. After all, she told herself, it would be a pity not to see all she could of this historic old port. She had been too anxious to see Beth and the baby on her previous visit and had seen little except lakes, trees and prairies on the way to Edmonton, though Beth had shown her slides and National Film Board movies of the Rocky Mountains 'in the meantime' as she had phrased it. Flora had not mentioned her unhappy conviction that there would be no other visit for her, but perhaps because of this feeling Flora had been totally enthralled by the majesty and grandeur of the lakes and snow-covered peaks and had asked to see them again and again.

Now she planned to transfer her notes to her new diary, have a warm bath and relax in bed with the television for company. This was still a novelty to her, for in South Africa the authorities were not permitting unlimited television. Their aim, ultimately, was to have programs in Afrikaans, English, and Bantu languages. This required a long time to arrange, as everyone there knew it would. She must make sure her room had a colour TV set, for this would be her treat tonight. She was to meet Martin in England in about a week, but she refused to think about that now.

She shifted her handbag onto her other arm and entered the lobby of an elegantly furnished hotel.

16

MARTIN unpacked his bags and placed his belongings neatly in the hotel drawers and wardrobe, then sat down on the edge of the bed and reached for the telephone. He was tired after the long flight from Edmonton and the hair-raising drive by taxi from Heathrow Airport, but he had been waiting too long for this moment to think about resting now.

"I'd like to place an overseas call to South Africa, please," he said as the operator answered. "The number is Cape Town 2-5821 and it's to Dr. Anthea Curtis. Thank you. Yes. I'm Dr. Nolan in Room 499. Is there a delay? Thank you."

He replaced the receiver and sat looking through the narrow sash window at a mural of roofs and chimney pots executed in red and grey, futuristic and three-dimensional, set against a wall of pale sky. Tucked in the lower left hand corner lay a small section of Hyde Park, the young green of the freshly washed trees in vivid contrast, yet restful to the eye. He turned his attention to the newspaper, but he was too excited to read.

If Anthea's schedule had remained unchanged, she should be at home, but would she be pleased to hear his voice? It seemed decades, not weeks, since he had last seen her. He had asked her to marry him, to spend the rest of her life with him, yet he found it difficult to recall the details of her face! It was almost as though she was slipping slowly away from him like some phantom figure gliding through tendrils of mist.

He gave a start as the telephone rang shrilly and the newspaper fell to the floor.

"Hello!" he said, excitement pitching his voice a tone higher than usual.

"Your call, Dr. Nolan."

"Thank you. Hello?"

A thin voice came through the earpiece.

"Dr. Curtis speaking."

Was that Anthea? Had her voice always sounded so cool?

"Anthea?"

"Martin! Is it really you? Where are you?"

"In London."

"London! Oh, how wonderful of you to phone me! And the Congress?"

"That starts tomorrow. I've only this minute arrived."

"You darling! It must have been awful to leave the family. And how was everyone in Canada?"

"The baby is gorgeous! Everyone well, except Flora."

The seconds passed in silence. Martin sensed that Anthea had frozen momentarily. Then softly she said, "When do you sail?"

"In just over a week."

"So you will soon be back. I've missed you terribly. Have you missed me, too?"

"Of course, sweetheart."

"I've been miserable. I don't know why I was so mean to you, and on our last night together! I've been hating myself ever since. Am I forgiven?"

"There's nothing to forgive."

Her words had cheered him but a sudden feeling of dejection robbed him of some of the joy. She's turning on the charm now, he thought, but then he was far enough away not to be troublesome.

"I've been wondering," he said. "Have you answered that fellow yet? Dave — Michael — whatever his name is?"

"Not finally. I'm terrified of doing the wrong thing but I'll have to cable him shortly. There is not much time and there are dozens of formalities if we are to be married. It isn't fair to keep him waiting like this."

"Anthea — please wait for me, darling! This is a serious matter. You can't possibly make a snap decision when your future is at stake. When I arrive we can talk it over."

"But there's no sense in waiting is there? All I'd be waiting for is to see you back with your wife. I don't think I could stand it! I need to get away — and quickly! The voyage to Australia will be a holiday for me and maybe help to put you out of my mind."

"You seem very anxious to do that," he retorted. "I'll never be able to forget you. I don't want to try! How can you want to blot me out of your thoughts like this? You still love me, don't you?"

"You know I do!"

"Well then — please don't do anything in a hurry. Flora may let me go, something may happen. Wait until I get back, promise me!"

"But Martin! You must realize I can't possibly promise! I have to think of myself now. If I can't have the love I want, maybe I should settle for something else. A career in a new country, perhaps, will make up in some way . . . "

Her voice trailed away thinly into silence. The line went dead.

Martin jiggled the phone up and down in exasperation but all he heard was a distant crackling. He dropped the hand piece onto its cradle and sat staring at it. He should not have called her, he told himself. He had meant to guide her but instead he probably had pushed her into making a wrong decision. He had tried to tell her that he would be free, but she had not really understood. How could she?

He rose and paced restlessly around the room. What and whom did Anthea want? The status of being married or the man himself? And then, which man? She had said she loved him, but would she love him if she found out he had killed his wife so as to be free to marry her? Would she love him then?

As he asked himself these questions the dejection seemed to be pressing down on him, trying to smother him, for in his heart he knew the answers. Maybe Anthea loved him in her way, or thought she did, but it was a small way at present. He knew it would have to be a much bigger thing if she were to make him happy. He wanted no little philandering, no trifling love from her. He wanted it all!

All of a sudden he laughed, but there was no mirth in the sound. In the stillness the echoes came mockingly back to him, reverberating from the furniture, laughing at him. My God! he thought. And what if she married the other fellow after all and I discover I've committed the 'perfect crime' too late?

He flung open the door, let it slam behind him and strode down the corridor to the lift. He suddenly could not bear to be alone. He needed a stiff drink — and a loose woman too — neither of which he had wanted to touch for a long time.

Some while later, more relaxed, he sat back in a low easy chair in a dimly lit fashionable bar lounge and let the hum of conversation roll over him. It felt good to be a nonentity for once, lost in a wilderness of disinterested humanity. He could even live it up a bit and no one would care a damn!

His hand was not quite steady as he lifted his glass to his lips and fastidiously eyed the expensively clad, bare-backed possibilities — those unescorted feline creatures always so readily available, if one knew where to look. He hated them, every goddam one of them, and he hated himself for wanting them, but this time dreams would not suffice.

He rose, straightened his tie, and approached.

17

THE old *Glenconnor*, immaculate in her gleaming coat of newly applied paint, sailed serenely from the dock to the open sea and southward into the English Channel. To Martin she seemed to be travelling slowly, like a mother duck gliding among her ducklings on a tranquil pond. He wanted to hurry her along — hurry the days — for his mind seemed to be floundering in rapids instead of steering calmly toward the far shore. He did not like it. He had always been so sure of himself.

He felt he had not handled Beth too successfully and now there were other worries.

For one, Anthea had seemed bent on marrying her young surgeon. It might be more difficult than he had thought to persuade her to change her mind.

For another, he was concerned that the porthole might not be large enough to allow Flora's body to be pushed through with ease. To push too hard might leave incriminating marks which must be avoided at all costs. Flora, fortunately, had lost a great deal of weight since leaving South Africa. This was not surprising considering her diet, for the most part, of clear tea and dry toast, but Martin was unhappy. He knew he would have to dispose of her body completely so that no damning post-mortem examination could be performed.

A further problem was his wife. Flora had not been behaving in her usual manner, and this disturbed Martin more than anything.

For administering the fatal drugs he had relied on Flora's drinking bouts, but she did not appear to have touched a drop of alcohol since the night before his arrival in Edmonton. An intoxicated Flora would be easy to dose, but with no symptoms requiring the use of sleeping pills, tranquilizers, or antacids, and a sober Flora, he knew his task would be well nigh impossible. Somehow she would have to be convinced that she would benefit from a protein supplement, for — after all — that was what the red gelatine capsules were, for the treatment of a protein deficiency. The only difference would be that he would substitute his two deadly drugs, as planned, one in each side of the capsule, immediately before giving it to Flora. And if Flora refused the capsule? What then? Could he wait for her to fall asleep and strangle her before she had time to cry out?

A small thought disturbed him. He stared unseeingly at the ocean before him. Was Anthea worth killing for? Would he live through weeks of agony to find her feelings for him superficial and valueless? He turned away and in a melancholy mood went down to the cabin to change into more comfortable clothes. He was relieved that there would be no tedious dressing for dinner this evening and glad he would not have to make polite conversation with his wife across the dinner table. Flora was already in her berth.

* * *

During the voyage Martin remained aloof avoiding any passengers who seemed inquisitive or over-friendly. He wanted no prying into his affairs. Most of his time was spent reading in the lounge, watching the games, and stepping out briskly along the decks for exercise, while Flora spent a good deal of time in the cabin lying down quietly on her berth reading, staring at the low ceiling, or on her knees looking glumly out of the porthole. She seemed to prefer having light snacks brought to her by the steward, rather than tidying herself for meals in the dining salon and Martin was glad of this. It gave him an opportunity of dropping a word here and there that his wife was not well and was to see a specialist when they arrived home. He managed also to insinuate that she was very depressed and felt he had made a good start toward his objective.

The days passed slowly and as they rounded the bulge of Africa the weather became sultry and oppressive. For several nights Martin tossed on his berth, the whirring of the ineffectual air conditioner more annoying than the heat. Flora, too, seemed restless and took to going up on deck at bedtime, returning later and later each succeeding night. Merely curious at first Martin gave it little thought but then a little idea inched itself into his mind. Was she . . . could she possibly be . . . meeting someone in the early hours, right under his nose?

At bedtime the following night he lay down on his berth, fully clothed, as if too tired to undress for the moment. Out of half closed eyes he watched his wife get up, run a brush through her hair, pick up her purse, and leave the cabin.

Martin waited for several minutes before going in search of her. He walked many times around the decks on each level. He searched all the reception rooms in the entire ship, but there was no sign of her. Annoyed, he returned to the cabin. As he opened the door he saw, to his surprise, that Flora was already in bed.

Martin undressed by the dim light that filtered through the opaque fanlight, then he crept over and stood looking down at her. Her eyes were wide open. She was staring at him in the half dark. A sick loathing rose in his throat.

"Where have you been?" he snapped ominously, but Flora continued to stare at him without speaking.

"I asked you a question," he repeated, enunciating each word carefully. "Where did you go?"

Flora sat up, putting out her hand to the bedside light switch and bathing the cabin in yellow light. Husband and wife glared challengingly at each other, then Flora smiled.

"Does it really matter after all these years? YOU ask ME, but I should be asking YOU! Where have YOU been? It's almost two o'clock! Isn't that rather late for someone who has a faithful girl friend waiting back home? Or is it that Anthea is not being faithful? Am I right? Were you searching for other game already?"

At her words, something seemed to click in Martin's brain. Flora's arched neck seemed tantalizingly vulnerable. Before he could stop himself his hands were around her throat.

"You leave Anthea out of this, do you hear?" he hissed, shaking her until he felt her neck would break and all the while his fingers were pressing, pressing, into her thin flesh. He felt her struggling frantically to free herself, clawing at his hands, and then reach up sideways with one arm. The service bell was beneath her first finger. Before he could make a move to stop her she had pushed it and was keeping her finger on it.

In a flash sanity returned. Martin released his hold abruptly and Flora fell heavily back on the pillow, gasping and choking as her breath struggled for entry to her lungs. She lay still a moment, then slowly she sat up and looked at Martin.

"So it has come to this!" she said sadly, her voice hoarse and unnatural. "You could have killed me!"

As she spoke there was a loud knock on the door and a voice called out, "Is everything all right in there?"

Martin swung around. "Of course!" he shouted irritably, but Flora had called 'Come in' and a steward opened the door. On the threshold he hesitated, his eyes scanning the scene. They took in Martin, in his pyjamas, poised beside his wife's bed and glaring indignantly at his intrusion, then came to rest on Flora leaning well away from her husband, resting on one elbow and rubbing her neck with one hand.

"Mrs. Nolan, are you all right? Did

you press your bell?" he asked, stepping inside.

Flora nodded as she sat slowly up and tidied the bed covers.

"Thank you for coming," she said hoarsely. "I'm most grateful. My husb . . . It was my neck but I think I'll be fine now." As she spoke she kept her eyes on Martin who stood like a mad man, breathing heavily but obviously keeping a firm grip on his temper.

The steward shrugged his shoulders and stepped back. Then, keeping his hand on the door knob, he looked at Martin. He started to say something but stopped and turned again to Flora.

"If you need me again, Mrs. Nolan, just press the buzzer and I'll be right here!"

"Thank you."

Martin, almost shivering with rage, turned on his heel and strode off toward the bathroom. Whatever must the man think of him? He had been made to look a fool and knew he had lost the round to Flora — damn her! It was a new experience and he was furious, furious with his wife but more furious with himself! It was the sort of behaviour one might expect in a cheap novel and if he had killed her then he would have ruined everything!

As he picked up his toothbrush he heard Flora say, "Would it be possible for me to move to another cabin?"

"Of course. No trouble in First Class, Mrs. Nolan," came the reply.

"Good. I'll think about it. Thank you. Good night."

"Just as you wish. Good night."

When Martin heard the cabin door close he returned to find Flora sitting as he had left her. Still seething, he glared at her and she looked steadily back at him.

"You fool!" he growled. "You utter fool to press the bell like that!"

She did not answer, but her eyes filled with tears. He tidied away his underclothes and climbed into bed. As he turned to face the wall he heard her lie down, but she made no move to turn off the light beside her berth.

She knows there will be no more sleep for her this night, he thought, and probably none for me either! Each would be staring ahead until well after dawn, with heads pounding and thoughts spinning. He realized too that, after all this, Flora still had not told him where she had been!

In the stillness the distant throb of the engines seemed to echo the blood pulsating through his body as he lay there — boof-BOOM, boof-BOOM. What had got into him to make him lose control the way he had? His sudden flash of rage had been so unlike him. At one time he had not even been aware of what he had been doing! He felt his heart beats quicken and placed his finger on his pulse in alarm. As he did so, he heard a hoarse whisper, "Are you awake?"

"Yes," he answered, startled.

There was a rustle of Flora's bedclothes and the next instant she was beside his berth.

"What is it?" he asked sharply.

She stood silently for a while and then she said, "I'm sorry! I suppose I was trying to hurt you. I didn't realize you'd take it like that. You weren't really trying to kill me, were you?"

Martin did not answer and after a few

minutes she went on.

"We have to talk, Martin. You understand that, don't you? We can't go on like this! Something is bound to snap. As things are I think it will be your sanity!" She moved a step closer and Martin turned his head to look up at her. She seemed but nineteen in her white nightgown with a ring of amber light shining behind her. Remembering a time in the past his jaw set grimly. What was she scheming this time?

"You'd like that, wouldn't you?" he snapped. "With me locked away you'd be free — really free — to mess around!"

For answer she sat down on the edge of his berth.

"You can't hurt me any more," she said softly. "I seem now to be able to view things from the outside, almost as if I were watching another me going through the motions of living. Why didn't you tell me I had a diseased liver? Why wasn't something done to help me? Do you hate me so much?"

Martin made no reply and she continued.

"I thought you found it convenient to

be married, perhaps, and did not really want me to leave. If things have changed, can't we talk about it? If you are serious about Anthea, I won't stand in your way, I promise, especially if I haven't much time. What do you want me to do?"

What did she mean — 'if I haven't much time'?

He sat up quickly. He seemed unable to breathe. He put out a hand, as if for help, then fell back as a sharp pain pierced his chest and left arm. It felt like a dagger turning and twisting inside him. He writhed in agony, possessed by a deep fear that clutched at his throat.

"My God! I can't stand it!" he whispered. But presently the pain eased and he lay panting, shattered and weak. Everything around him seemed far away as if viewed through the wrong end of a telescope. He felt Flora's thin hands groping for his and then, as if from a great distance, he heard her say, "Martin! Are you all right?" She was rubbing his numb hand between her own.

"Can you hear me? It's Flora! Martin! Please, what is it?"

Martin shook his head as if to clear it

and beads of perspiration broke out on his forehead. He could not have spoken at that moment if he had tried, for his jaws seemed to be locked together. He lifted his hand to the side. Flora, apparently understanding at once, opened the bedside drawer. She lifted out his small travelling medical case and held it before him so that he could look inside. As she systematically pointed to each container he shook his head but presently she chose the correct box. Martin nodded with relief as he held out his hand for one and placed it carefully under his tongue.

He saw by the sudden look of fear in her eyes that the truth had dawned on her, just as he too began to realize the full implications.

He turned his face to the wall away from Flora. He could not bear to look at her. He waved his hand for her to leave him, but when she walked over to her bunk and lay down, he felt comforted. Life was altogether too complicated. He shut his eyes.

18

FLORA had not realized the gravity of the situation until Martin took the tablet to relieve his pain. For a moment she had not known whether to call back the steward or go in search of a doctor. At that hour she had been reluctant to call anyone unless absolutely necessary. She knew she might still have to, but for the present she was content to keep watch over him, even though he did not want her there.

Her thoughts scattered and fell in disarray as she lay down on her berth to begin her vigil. That it was serious she knew, and that it might come again, be even worse, that he might die. The very idea made her gasp. She had always been so helpless, depending on him to arrange the minutest detail for her. She would be lost. She knew she could not face being alone for long.

"Maybe it will not be for long," she murmured. If her jaundice and nausea meant a liver complaint or even cancer, she wanted to know. Suddenly it was of the utmost importance to find out.

'I'll see the doctor first thing in the morning, the very first thing!' she promised herself. This she had labelled 'Priority No. 2' in her plan of action and it was long overdue.

Some hours later, feeling rather hollow-eyed and grim, Flora propped herself up on one elbow to pour out her early morning tea. Martin stirred and turned over. Bewilderment flashed momentarily in his eyes as he looked across at her.

Flora climbed out of her bed, poured out a cup of tea and held it for him to drink. He took a few sips, as if parched, and slid back beneath the blanket, but his eyes did not leave her face.

From the bathroom she fetched a face cloth wrung out in warm, soapy water and sponged his face and hands.

"You are ill," she said, then, stating the fact as if their positions were reversed and she the doctor. Martin nodded.

"Can I get you anything?" she asked.

"Please. More cold water."

Flora returned to the bathroom, rinsed

and filled the tumbler with fresh water and handed it to him. He swallowed a little slowly, returned the glass to her and lay down again, shutting his eyes.

"Shall I call the doctor?" she asked.

"No. No. I'm much better . . . Thank you."

The last words had been a reluctant uttering of an obvious afterthought that Flora had to smile. She replaced the case, collected her clothes and stepped into the bathroom. When she returned Martin was sound asleep.

Quietly she tiptoed over to him and stood looking down at the still-youthful face, the fine contours of the coldly aristocratic profile. Now, more than ever, they seemed chiselled from marble.

Was this really the Martin who had almost choked her not so long ago? She felt no anger now, no hatred, only sadness at the wasted years. Happiness had been such a casual visitor! If she helped him now, would she be laying herself open to more of the same harsh treatment or had there been a flicker of kindness in his eyes as he sipped his tea?

Flora turned away and a short while later was up on the cool deck chewing slowly at the salty crackers she had brought with her. A few passengers out for their early morning exercise greeted her and she greeted them in return, though absentmindedly. It felt good to be out of doors after the long hours in the stuffy cabin, but she was too tired to walk around. The sea air stung her chapped skin as a fresh breeze whipped along the deck flapping noisily at the deck chairs and light clouds misting up from the horizon diffused the warmth of the sun's morning rays. Chilled, Flora went down to the cabin for her jacket and found Martin still sleeping soundly. It seemed pointless to resume her watch over him, and she did not wish to waken him by the probable clatter of breakfast dishes if she ate in the cabin. Slowly she moved along the passageway and down the stairs to the dining saloon.

As she seated herself in her seldom-occupied chair the cheery voice of the table steward rang out, "Good morning, Mrs, Nolan. You are feeling better now I hope?"

"A little, thank you," she answered without warmth, not caring for his unctuous breed. She watched him flick fussily at the immaculate cloth and spotless cutlery, then she added, "My husband is not well today."

"I am sorry to hear that! I hope he will be over it soon."

"Thank you," she replied, noting that he had sounded genuinely sorry. Flora felt ashamed of her coolness toward him. He was, after all, only trying to be pleasant, a part of his job. She smiled at him, then turned her attention to the elaborate menu.

At each item she shuddered mentally. 'Orange Juice — Fried Eggs — Grilled Ham or Bacon — Sausages — Fried Liver and Onions'! The list went on interminably. Why had she bothered to come to breakfast? Then she read 'Grilled Breakfast Steak.' Maybe she could try a small portion, well done and completely fat free. She gave her order and sat back in her chair. Curious stares and half smiles were directed her way and she realized she was inviting comment by coming in to a meal. The tinge to her skin, though slightly faded, was still an embarrassment to her. She bent forward to crumble a breadroll, and when her breakfast arrived she cut it into tiny pieces and chewed slowly. When she had finished all she wanted she placed her knife and fork neatly together on her plate and, unconsciously squaring her shoulders, rose from the table. She felt ready now to face the doctor. She felt ready to face almost anything!

A short while later Flora was being ushered out of the doctor's consulting room by a plump, white-haired old man with a pronounced stoop.

"Then you will call this afternoon for the results, Mrs. Montgomery?" he asked and Flora nodded.

"Yes. Thank you, Doctor." She smiled at him.

He had been gentle and understanding but she was very much afraid that the whole examination had been a waste of time. He looked old and decrepit and she had lost confidence in any opinion before he had even expressed it, but this was partly her own fault. She had omitted to tell him the most vital information: that

Martin had given her two different kinds of pills in Edmonton, pills which in all probability had now been analyzed in Halifax. She had been to such pains not to mention Martin or to implicate him that, possibly she had made it impossible for the doctor to make any diagnosis, yet this was the reason for her visit to him.

He had taken the usual blood sample and asked for a specimen of her urine, as routine. His hands had moved carefully, exploring thoroughly, but she knew it had been a stupid mistake to keep quiet about the pills. She did not quite understand what had made her do it. Then too, she had given a false name and cabin number so as to be difficult to trace. This meant that she must return personally for the results or run the risk of being found out. She was suddenly tired of all the pretence and dishonesty.

With dragging feet she walked up and onto the deck to stare ahead at the vast expanse of blue-green sea that stretched into the distance to merge almost imperceptibly into the grey-blue sky. Seawater slapped angrily at the side of the ship. 'Stupid! Stupid!' it seemed to say and Flora knew she deserved it. She was to see the doctor again later in the day. Maybe she would tell him then. He should know all the facts before he gave a diagnosis. She owed it to him to see that he got them.

Impatiently she brushed her hair out of her eyes, blown there by a mounting wind, and made her way down to the cabin to see to Martin's needs.

19

MARTIN awoke to a grey day and the ship's erratic rolling and pitching. His first thought was that it was the fateful 13th of June. Through the porthole turbulent green water surged alongside spattering arcs of white spray before the wind but the next moment a swell caught the ship, carrying her on high and there was but a circle of overcast sky. He had relied on poor weather when planning Flora's D-Day and now, well satisfied with the obviously stormy conditions, he swung his legs purposefully over the edge of the berth.

In a flash Flora was beside him, her hand on his arm. "Be careful! Won't you have to take it easy for a while?"

Martin nodded dully as remembrance returned. How could he have forgotten? He drew back under the bedcovers and leaned against his pillow.

"What time is it?" he asked.

"Almost one-thirty."

"The morning's gone!"

He ran his hand thoughtfully along the fine stubble on his chin. Could he delay one more day or would last-night revellers interfere with his plans? He watched Flora pottering about with hot water and towels and submitted weakly to being sponged down, but all the while his mind was racing. A razor was placed in his hand and hardly conscious of his actions he ran the blades across his face.

"I'll see if I can find something for you to eat," he heard Flora say while tidying his bed clothes. "What would you like? A little soup?"

"Yes, please," he answered. "Nothing solid."

She left the cabin and returned shortly, followed by a steward bearing a tray.

"This has not been a very good voyage for either of you, has it?" the man said, lurching forward and setting down the tray with a thump as the ship rolled to starboard.

"No, it hasn't," Martin remarked disinterestedly, wishing he did not feel obliged to answer.

"And now the weather is taking a turn for the worse, they tell me," the steward continued. "Everything will have to be battened down before nightfall. Bed will be the best place for everyone. You should stay where you are, Doctor."

"Yes, I intend to," Martin replied, settling himself more comfortably as the steward left the cabin. It might be useful to let the man think he was remaining in bed should an alibi be needed after all. Feeling somewhat happier he allowed Flora to place a pillow behind his back, spread a napkin over his chest and hand him the bowl of steaming soup.

"Thank you," he said, strangely embarrassed at the unaccustomed attention. He watched her sit down on the side of her berth and fold her hands, then slowly he began to sip. From time to time he glanced surreptitiously across at her and noted the black rings under her eyes and her strange pallor. She seemed inordinately tired and old. His medical eye told him there was something very wrong with her to make her look as she did at the age of forty and a tiny twinge of guilt plucked at his conscience. She had been a stranger in South Africa, alone and at his mercy. He had been anything but kind to her over the years yet here she was, not at all well, but waiting to help him, wanting to help him, now that he was ill. He had shown little regard for her. He had, in fact, caused her to be sick by giving her pills to make her nauseated and was even now preparing to watch her die, if he carried out his plan.

But this is no time to be soft, he told himself firmly. It is in Flora's interests to appear solicitous now, of course! He lowered his spoon, wiped his mouth carefully and sat back.

"Did you realize that I probably had a slight coronary?" he asked as Flora rose to remove the bowl from his lap.

"Yes."

"Others could follow at any time — could even be fatal — but you know that too?"

Flora nodded and resumed her seat.

"This makes a difference," he said, running his hands across his hair in an almost womanly gesture. "It has shaken me more than I'd like to admit. I had not realized that the years had taken their toll of me. I was young, my best years still ahead. Now, suddenly, I want desperately to live — really live — before I die."

Flora did not speak but Martin noticed she had clenched her hands tightly together. He made a sudden split-second decision, a momentous decision, and shifted his position, stalling for time. He wanted no misunderstanding. His words must be precise.

"I want you to give me my freedom as soon as possible," he said at last, looking intently at her. "This means, of course, that you too will be free." He saw the colour flood her face and drain away, leaving the same slightly yellow pallor.

"So it is Anthea after all?" she whispered.

"Yes. You understand, don't you?"

"I'm not sure I do," she answered. "You have always seemed incapable of loving anyone, except perhaps Beth, and even that was not . . . " Flora broke off and Martin stared at her, thunderstruck. What was she trying to say?

"But they say love is a two-way street," she continued. "Does Anthea love you?"

"She says so."

"You don't sound convinced."

"It's too early to be sure."

Flora sighed. "Then it seems that she does not! But you must know that. Why aren't you facing up to it?"

Martin did not reply. Flora leaned closer, her knuckles showing white on her tightly clasped hands.

"You are making a mistake, Martin," she said earnestly. "You have always looked for the wrong things in life, or maybe the right things but at the wrong time. Someone like Anthea could be the answer, but surely you should know each other better, each decide that life would be impossible without the other to share it, before thinking of any permanent relationship. I thought you would have learned by now."

Martin continued to stare incredulously. Was Flora right? Had he sought the wrong things in life? And Anthea? Was she one of those things? But what right had Flora to talk to him this way? She had been responsible for most of his unhappiness, damn her! A slow anger rose in him, washing away the stirrings of warmth that he had felt momentarily for her. His mouth set sternly as he watched her stand up and walk over to him, her face twisted in a half smile.

"I've been guilty of many things," she sighed, "and I'm sorry, truly sorry. But I feel I've more than paid for them over these last years. You have been guilty too, but of different things. They are behind us now. Our score is even. Can't we make our peace with one another? We may not have long to live, either of us!"

Her lips quivered. She bent over, put out a hand and rested it lightly on his. "What do you want from me? What can I expect from you? Let us at least talk it over, settle our differences, forget Anthea for the moment."

Martin made no sign that he had noticed her gesture. He snarled suddenly, his voice hoarse with unusual emotion. "Forget Anthea? You are crazy! Don't you understand? She is everything I want in a woman — everything I should have had and that you denied me!"

Flora lifted her hand from his and straightened up as Martin continued.

"As I say, I WANT her, but I shall not get her unless I am free to marry her. Anthea has made that clear! I must be free soon or she will marry someone else — in July."

Flora sat down heavily at Martin's feet, her face the picture of amazement. "JULY! Are you telling me there's another man? That she's playing one of you against the other? You fool! Can't you see that all she wants is someone to push her higher up her little ladder of success?"

"Maybe, but I still want her!"

Flora threw up her hands, then laughed hysterically. "Well — I can't help you! No one can! Marry her then, if she wants you, but don't expect the world to change."

She rose shakily and stood a moment looking down at him.

"I won't stand in your way, as I said, and I really mean that," she added and Martin saw that tears trembled and then fell on to her cheeks but she made no move to wipe them away. "But there is not much time between now and July. How can you hope to be completely free in so short a time?"

She looked hard at him and suddenly her hand flew to her mouth.

Martin could see by the expression in her eyes that she understood.

"So I was not wrong after all," she breathed. "You weren't even planning to ask for a divorce! Divorces take time and that is something you don't have. Is that what you mean?"

Martin nodded. Flora drew back, one hand on her chest.

"Why are you telling me this now?" she asked, her eyes searching his.

"I hardly know! Perhaps it is because I'm not well. Perhaps because I know I can't go through with it as I planned."

"You can't go through with it as you planned!" she whispered incredulously.

He paused to let the full import of his words penetrate, then crisply and clearly came the rest.

"I'm asking you to leave me — now! I want Anthea to know as soon as the ship docks that we are no longer together — that our marriage is over."

"Asking me!" Flora said softly. "This is something new for you, isn't it? But you are not exactly in a position to threaten or bargain are you?"

She laughed again, her head thrown back like some wild creature. "The awful thing is that I probably shall do exactly as you say — just as I always have!"

She walked unsteadily to the doorway, then turned with her hand on the doorknob.

"But maybe there still is some justice somewhere in this rotten world! You said you could have another attack at any time and it could prove fatal. Perhaps it will come sooner than you think! Maybe even tonight! If it does I shall not be at hand to make things easy for you. You will have to face death alone. I'm through! But then that is what you want, isn't it?"

Her jaw quivered. She picked agitatedly at the beads on her small clutch purse, then moved slowly out of the cabin and closed the door, her back bent as though she carried a great burden.

Martin was left alone, listening to the

disturbing creaking of the ship as the waves swirled against her hull. The wind whistled relentlessly. It was a bleak day and he knew that a worse night was to come.

20

FOR some two hours Flora walked aimlessly around the ship, oblivious to the mounting anger of the storm. Her mind seemed narrowed in a groove. She could think only of Martin. That their marriage was over was something she had known for many years, but that he should have told her, though not in so many words, that he had planned to kill her, sent her pacing blindly with renewed horror. Just imagine! If he had not taken ill she might now, this very minute, be lying dead in the cabin or at the bottom of the ocean!

"He's mad!" she muttered to herself. "Completely mad!" She was lucky to be free, but free for what? What was there in life for her? An existence perhaps in some cold hotel room or lonely apartment waiting for death? And how long would that be?

Abruptly she turned on her heel and made her way haltingly towards the doctor's consulting rooms. She had said she would return later in the day. Perhaps the results of the tests would be ready now.

Approaching the young nurse at the reception desk a few minutes later, she said, "Doctor asked me to call this afternoon. I'm Flora Montgomery."

"Yes, Mrs. Montgomery. Doctor is expecting you. One moment please."

Flora settled herself in the nearest chair and picked up a magazine. She flipped the pages one by one, but her thoughts were a blur as she struggled to think clearly. Could she tell the doctor about the pills Martin had given her in Canada, or would it be best to wait and see whether he had been able to come up with a diagnosis and perhaps prognosis without having to implicate her husband? And should she tell the doctor about Martin's virtual admission? She toyed with the idea of getting even somehow with Martin, making him pay for all the years of misery he had caused her, but she abandoned it reluctantly. Who knew what repercussions there might be? To brand him a potential murderer (and to prove this might not be easy) could cause untold suffering to Beth and the baby. No! She could not hurt them!

She stared at the illustrated pages before her. What must she do? Submit meekly? Take it all lying down?

"Mrs. Montgomery! Mrs. Montgomery, are you all right?"

Flora looked up. She had for a moment forgotten. She must answer to that name here. A flush spread slowly across her face and down her neck as she struggled to her feet and the nurse smiled kindly.

"Doctor will see you now."

"Thank you," Flora murmured. "Please let me have my bill as I leave. I'd prefer to pay now and not involve the Purser's Office."

"Certainly, Mrs. Montgomery."

Seated at the doctor's desk she waited patiently while he opened the folder before him and glanced through the papers it contained. He shifted his glasses, leaned well back in his chair and cleared his throat. When he looked up she was afraid suddenly that what he had to tell her would not be good news. She felt her hands go limp and there was a singing of a tuning fork in her ears. She slid softly to the floor.

The doctor pressed a bell on the wall and moved around his desk with remarkable speed for his age to kneel beside Flora. As the nurse entered, he put his hands under Flora's shoulders, resting her head on his body.

"Help me lift her onto the couch," he said.

The nurse took Flora's ankles and together they lifted her and placed her on the examining couch. Flora opened her eyes.

"I'm sorry! That was silly of me!"

"There is nothing to be alarmed about. Just relax. That's better."

With a hand on Flora's pulse he turned to the nurse. "Thank you. I'll manage now," and with a nod she was dismissed.

It was a good half hour before a visibly shaken Flora emerged from the doctor's consulting rooms.

"Thank you, Doctor. I feel much better now."

"Take care of yourself and remember what I told you."

"Yes, I shall. Goodbye."

"Bye."

As the door closed behind him, Flora moved over to pay her bill, leaning on the nearest length of wall for support. Her legs could hardly support her, but she managed to open her bag and count out the required amount. She was determined not to stay a moment longer in the vicinity in case someone saw her, for she was Flora Montgomery to the doctor and nurse and wished no one else to know of her visit. Somehow she managed a weak 'thanks' and then she was groping her way down the gangway to the nearest lounge. Her heart was beating fast and she felt sick as she sank into a chair.

"Air! I must get some air!" she murmured, but one look at the mountainous waves outside drove her instead into a deserted washroom nearby.

Later, more composed but still somewhat shaken, she crept out and along the corridor in the opposite direction from her cabin. She had no plan. She knew only that she would not go back to the cabin and Martin

— could not go back — but there were two nights and one day to face before the ship docked in Table Bay.

'I must be alone to think,' her heart cried, but she knew that she was alone, quite alone, and that her mind was numb. She turned then and made her way slowly to the writing room off the Promenade Deck. This was where she had found sanctuary before, where she had been alone in the early hours to write in her diary. This should be her refuge now, but what of tomorrow?

The writing room was occupied by an elderly white-haired lady who was scratching laboriously with an old-fashioned nibbed pen. Flora crept by unnoticed to take up her usual position in the high-backed wing chair well hidden from the doorway.

She leaned back and eyed the blotter that lay before her. If only she could write in her diary, she thought, but she had left it in her large travelling handbag and had brought only her small purse. But maybe she would write anyway. Perhaps by so doing she would get a clearer picture of where she stood and where she was heading. She could even write to Jock.

Flora had promised herself that this was something she would never do, but the temptation to communicate with someone who would understand was overpowering. Yes, she thought. She would write to Jock and mail it to the ship's office address in Cape Town. If she did so, surely there could be no danger that his wife would ever see it or read it, especially if she marked it 'Personal and Confidential — to await arrival.'

She picked up the ballpoint pen that lay on the desk and drew towards her several sheets of writing paper with the ship's crest on them. She stared at them, trying to think lucidly and trying too to will her hands to stop shaking sufficiently for her to write legibly.

Presently, with a great sigh, she began to draw the pen across the paper. She wrote and wrote, pouring out all her thoughts, baring all her unhappiness, until a deep calm seemed to settle on her. It was as if Jock stood beside her now. He understood. He cared. A warmth seemed to seep through her body and she was comforted.

When she looked up the room was deserted. She bent forward to see outside but it was completely dark. Her wristwatch told her that it was 9 p.m. She felt empty but she knew she could not face food even if she were able to find any. She had no wish for anything. She leaned back in the chair and shut her eyes. The writing paper lay untidily on the desk blotter in front of her but she made no move to put it together neatly. Exhaustion overcame her and she fell asleep with her head set at an awkward angle in the wing of the high chair.

Several hours later she awoke, her neck stiff and sore, and felt chilled. She looked at the sheets before her, then with a decisive movement she pulled an envelope towards her and wrote in big letters on the front. She stuffed the papers inside it, turned over the flap, licked it and firmly stuck it down, then affixed a stamp. As she did so, depression seemed to wash over her. She put her head in her hands and let the tears flow as they would. Why not, she thought. There was no one here to see her grief.

When she rose finally, there was a calmness in her soul she had not known in years. She picked up her small purse and the envelope and walked slowly through the deserted ship toward the Purser's Office, unmindful of the changing angles of the floor beneath her feet. For some time she stood looking at the ship's box before she dropped the envelope inside and as she did so a part of her seemed to go with it, winging across the waves to the arms of Jock.

Tears welled up again to sting her eyes. She had bared her very soul, yet she was not even sure that Jock would remember her. It did not seem possible that one could be close in body and mind one minute and eons of time away the next. She had thought of writing to Beth, but fear of a coldly hostile and superior Arthur perhaps reading her letter, held her back. And there was no one else — no one in the whole vast world! Had anyone ever been so alone and friendless?

Blindly she crept to the heavy doors that shielded the reception rooms from the wind and rain and held them open as a rush of wind nearly lifted her off her feet. Then, with legs almost buckling under her, she climbed over the sill onto the deck, inhaling great breaths of cold air. As she allowed the doors to slam shut after her, a burst of fine spray hurtled towards her. It trickled slowly down her neck. She shivered but made no attempt to wipe it away.

With one hand outstretched for support, she stumbled a short way along the deck, then stopped abruptly to lean against the metal stairway as another burst of spray hurled itself at her. In sudden light it rose, as if reaching out to her, then it fell limply back to the dark chasm of night beyond. It seemed to be saying something to her and she smiled. She was getting fanciful! Why, even the prayer she had noticed earlier in the doctor's examination room had seemed to take on a special meaning. It was the frame that had first impressed her but then, as she lay quietly on the couch, she had read the words. She had read them over and over again. The doctor had noticed her reading them and had smiled at her.

'Wonderful words,' he had said. 'They

have been an inspiration to countless thousands, I imagine — perhaps millions — since they first were uttered in 1934 by Reinhold Niebuhr in Massachusetts.'

Flora had nodded politely, not quite understanding about the millions, but she had tried to commit the words to memory. What were they?

> 'Oh God, give us serenity to accept what cannot be changed,
> courage to change what should be changed
> and wisdom to distinguish the one from the other'

Yes, that was right, or almost so, but she wondered why, suddenly, she should want to talk to God. For years she had felt He had forsaken her, so why now should she ask Him for anything? Serenity? A lovely word, mellow and warm! Her lips were chattering as the icy wind pierced through the flimsy fabric of her jacket.

A deckhand hurried by, shielding his face against the wind-swept spray. He was looking out to sea and did not notice the small figure in the dark pantsuit who stood in the shadows as black as the starless night. He was intent only on checking that all was well and that everything was fastened securely before the storm's worst fury struck.

Flora watched him go by with something akin to pity in her heart. He is young, she thought. He has still to face life with its delusions and disappointments, to tread the paths of dreams crushed underfoot like shells along the shore, washed by sand and tide. Thank God my life is almost over!

21

WHEN Flora left him, Martin stared at the closed door that had closed too on a chapter of his life. She had gone, as he had asked, but for a moment he felt no relief, no concern, nothing. He tried to think of Anthea but she remained distant, a dim figure lost in a void of his memory, and was no comfort to him. He turned toward the bedside drawer, leaned over to remove some pills and set them in neat array on the table top. He did not like to be alone when he was ill, he never had. The sight of Jackson's smiling black face would have been more than welcome, but he too was distant. Martin sighed and turned over.

All afternoon he dozed fitfully and by evening he was too wide awake to sleep further. He tossed this way and that, each fold in the rumpled sheet pressing relentlessly into his back. A savage wind howled and whistled through the ship, and Martin knew there would be no more rest for him that night. He picked up a book and commenced to page through it.

In the early hours the porthole over Flora's berth suddenly flew open and a blast of cold air spattered salt spray across the cabin. Startled, Martin climbed out of his berth, crossed the narrow floor space to the empty berth, kneeled on the bedcover and slammed the porthole shut. Strangely shaken by the effort, he padded back to his bed and huddled under the bedclothes. Morning seemed another world away.

It was then, for the first time, that he began to wonder about Flora. Where had she gone? Why had she not taken her night clothes and toothbrush? He remembered the look on her face as she said 'You weren't even planning to ask for a divorce!' and the way her jaw had quivered. He thought too of her yellow pallor and bent back as she turned to leave the cabin, and he was not proud of himself. With a gesture of irritation he threw back the blankets and climbed out of bed.

'You will have to face death alone,' Flora had said. 'I'm through. But then that is what you want, isn't it?'

He was about to pace the floor, but fear of a recurrence of the agonizing pain he had suffered forced him to abandon the idea. He sighed, then climbed back into his berth. He most certainly did not want to 'face death alone' as Flora had put it, yet he had asked her to leave him! He could call for a doctor but that would have to be in the morning. The ship's doctor would not be pleased to be called in the early hours when the worst was already over and in any case he would prefer to ask his friend Tom Meyer as soon as he docked. He would have every facility at hand at Groote Schuur Hospital, whereas the ship's equipment was bound to be somewhat inferior.

Feeling miserably cold and hungry, morose and neglected, he managed to get through the remainder of the long night until at last the welcome rattle of cups on saucers heralded the morning tray.

"Morning, Doctor Nolan! Dreadful storm wasn't it?" the steward remarked brightly as he entered. "The worst is over though," he added, setting down Martin's tray.

"Good," Martin grunted. "I've not had much sleep."

"And your wife? Did she not sleep either?" the man asked, noticing the empty berth.

"I don't really know," Martin replied, stifling a yawn. "She didn't come back to bed. I've not been well, you know. I didn't want to be tossing and turning and keeping her awake. She most probably asked for another cabin."

A worried frown appeared on the steward's brow. "Not as far as I know," he said, "but I'll ask about it. Come to think of it, I haven't seen Mrs. Nolan since yesterday afternoon." He paused a moment, then cocked his head slightly to one side.

"You don't think anything could have happened to her?"

"No. No! She told me she was not coming back," Martin answered.

The steward scratched his chin but all he said was, "I hope you're right, sir."

Martin's jaw twitched with anger, but he picked up his teacup and drank as though he had not heard. The steward watched him a moment then looked across at the empty berth, seemed to make a mental note of the slight indentations in the bedcover and traces of wetness, but he said no more. A few seconds later he had gone, bearing Flora's tray with him.

Martin leaned back against his pillow, his face the picture of annoyance. He realized that Flora's departure was bound to cause a few raised eyebrows, and suddenly he wished that they had never left South Africa. Why had he not been content to let things alone? His life had been orderly, his work progressive. Why had he allowed himself to become infatuated? No woman was worth it! Not even Anthea! It had been the youthful figure of loveliness that had captivated him, for he suspected now that Anthea, the woman, was selfish, spoiled and conceited, her love for him a mere sham.

Dully he gazed at the dismal grey of morning visible through the porthole and watched it change little by little to a brighter shade of blue. Along with the sky Martin's spirits lifted and by noon, ravenously hungry and decidedly more cheerful, he ordered a light meal to be sent to him. He was enjoying it at his leisure when there was a loud rap on the door.

"Come in," he called, and to his surprise the Chief Steward entered. Martin eyed him with distrust.

"Yes?" he asked sharply.

"I wanted to see your wife, sir. Do you know where I can find her?"

Astonished at the unexpected interest in Flora, Martin could only gape at him.

"Not at the moment," he said at last. "Can I help you?"

The man seemed to consider this for several seconds, then he spoke.

"Perhaps it would be best if I spoke to you."

"Yes?"

"I understand you have not yet seen your wife today?"

"That is right."

"Well — we've been checking since early morning and we cannot find her. She does not appear to have been seen since late yesterday afternoon."

"Really? There is possibly some very simple explanation. My wife likes to be alone and there must be many corners tucked away in an old ship like this. But, as I told the steward earlier, she was intending to ask for another cabin."

"Yes, sir. So I understand."

"I have already explained all this! I've been ill and so has my wife. She was told there would be no difficulty in obtaining another cabin."

The man nodded, as though weighing the matter, then he half-turned as it to go and stopped.

"Well," he added, looking over his shoulder, "if you do see your wife, please ask her to call at the Purser's Office. He has the radiogram she was expecting."

"The radiogram?"

"Yes. It was received during the night."

"For my wife?" Martin's voice was incredulous.

"Yes."

"But, why didn't the Purser give it to me?"

"It was addressed to your wife

personally. He has no authority to give it to anyone else at present."

"But this is ridiculous!" Martin exploded. "I should have given it to her as soon as she returned."

"Yes, Doctor. That is what WE shall do, most probably. And now, if you will excuse me — I must get on with my duties."

He nodded coolly and walked stiffly away, the epitome of naval discipline.

A perplexed Martin stared after him. What was this radiogram that Flora had been expecting and where was she? Icy sweat broke out along his backbone. She had said she would leave him and she had, but now he would have to go in search of her when he should be resting in bed. He was being subjected to unpleasant questioning and he did not like it! He felt suddenly as though a steam-roller pressed relentlessly behind him down a hill. He knew he would have to run faster or it would roll right over him, but his legs seemed almost paralysed.

"This is some macabre nightmare!" he told himself, but he knew that it was reality and something he would have to face.

Peevishly he pushed the remains of his meal to one side. His appetite had completely vanished.

22

"WOULD Mrs. Martin Nolan kindly report to the Purser's Office on D Deck. Thank you."

Martin heard the announcement as he paced systematically through the ship. It was repeated at regular intervals for some while and each time he heard the crackling of the loud-speakers preparatory to the broadcast, his muscles tensed. He kept telling himself it would be the best thing that could happen to him if Flora had vanished (for that, after all, had been his goal) but he was not entirely convinced. Something was very wrong — something he did not understand. One did not fade into oblivion on board ship.

Had there been an accident? Could Flora, not feeling well, have gone outside for air and been swept over the side during the storm? A picture flashed into his mind, a vivid picture of pale hands beating frantically as a deep swell washed over them and they were gone. He shuddered and knew then that he would never have been able to watch Flora drown, no matter how much he despised and hated her. The way he had planned it, her death would have been instantaneous, or nearly so. The fast acting drugs would have killed her in seconds once the capsule dissolved. She would have hit the water without a sound and without knowing anything about it — if he had been able to go through with it, which he now very much doubted, for it was one thing to plan a murder and quite another to commit one.

A sudden thought caught him in mid-stride. The drugs! What if questions were asked? He had placed the two deadly drugs, together with the gelatine capsules, with his other medicines in his medical case. It would never do to have them around if his cabin were to be searched. Urgent purpose lending wings to his feet, he hurried back the way he had come.

On reaching his cabin, he opened the door and walked straight across to the bedside table. The aspirin, anti-coagulant and pain-reliever containers lay where he had left them earlier. He opened the drawer and looked inside. He drew it to its furthest limit, then in a sudden frenzy he removed the entire drawer, but there was no mistake. His medical case, with contents, had gone.

A movement at the door caused him to look up. The Purser's interested eyes were watching him through the doorway. Angrily Martin slammed the drawer shut.

"Yes?" he asked. "What is it?"

"Excuse me, Doctor," the man said. "Captain Anderson sends his compliments and requests that you see him in Cabin 91."

Martin looked at him uncomprehendingly, then nodded dully. Something had told him that this was coming, yet when it did he was unprepared. He looked vaguely around him, then turned to the Purser.

"What is it, do you know?" he asked.

The man's eyebrows rose inquiringly. "I've no idea, sir."

Martin nodded again, angry that in his anxiety he had asked a stupid question. He seemed unable to think clearly. He ran a hand over his hair, then adjusted his tie and shirt sleeves, but the actions were automatic. As he followed the Purser along the corridor he could not rid himself of the feeling that he was being led, slowly and inexorably, to his execution.

Some minutes later the Purser tapped on a door. A voice called "Come in" and when Martin entered he found himself in the presence of a man of Napoleonic stature and bearing who rose from his leather chair and advanced with outstretched hand. "Good evening, Dr. Nolan. I'm sorry that I had to ask you to see me."

Hostile and wary Martin shook the proffered hand and waited for the Captain to continue.

"Please be seated."

"No, thank you."

The Captain shrugged his shoulders and turned away. "I see you do not want any beating around the bush! I don't blame you. I shall come to the point, but first of all, would you like a drink?"

"No, thank you."

The Captain nodded, then slid back into his chair and crossed one short leg over the other. He picked up his glass, drained it completely and placed it carefully in its coaster as if it were of the utmost importance to be dead in the centre. Finally he looked up, his sharp black eyes seemingly piercing Martin's soul.

"What we say to each other is 'off the record' as they say! I want you to understand. There is no hidden microphone or anything of that nature."

He smiled as if to soften the blow of what was to follow, but Martin stood stiffly before him with no sign that he had heard.

"Your wife's disappearance is most distressing to us all, as you will understand. We have searched diligently throughout the ship and I am sorry to have to inform you that if Mrs. Nolan is not found by the time we dock tomorrow, it must be presumed that she has been lost at sea. There will, of course, have to be an Inquiry."

Martin could only nod once more.

The Captain continued.

"The crew and I have a certain responsibility toward our passengers to see that no harm comes to them. I, personally, am directly responsible to my superiors. I shall be questioned and, as you must realize, I shall do my best to prove that there was no negligence on our part."

He uncrossed his legs and stood up, puffing out his chest as if trying to make himself appear larger and taller, and began to strut across the carpet.

Martin's eyes followed each step.

"There was a storm last night, as you know," the man went on. "Few passengers would have ventured out on deck and we find it hard to believe Mrs. Nolan would have done so. Certainly no one appears to have seen her at any time. Can you perhaps throw any light on her movements last night?"

He stopped suddenly abreast of Martin and peered into his face. A slow anger began to rise in Martin's chest.

"No, I'm sorry!" he replied icily. "My wife was with me yesterday when I ate my lunch and I have not seen her since. That is all I know."

"I see," the Captain said softly. He clasped his hands behind his back and proceeded once again to pace the floor.

"I understand you and your wife had not been on the best of terms during this trip," he added. "And perhaps before that?"

A hot flush mounted slowly to suffuse Martin's face but he did not reply.

"One of my stewards has a report that I feel might look rather damaging in a court of law," the man went on, "but I wonder if you realize quite how damaging?"

"What the devil do you mean?" Martin exploded, the muscles in his cheek twitching dangerously.

The Captain eyed him coolly.

"I thought you would understand," he said, his lips twisting in a smirk. "Surely you have not forgotten that your wife found it necessary to summon a steward in the early hours of the thirteenth?"

"How dare you!" Martin thundered, but the Captain ignored the interruption.

"I am trying my best to impress upon you how serious your position will be if your wife does not appear — that is all!" he stated, sitting down again. He folded his arms across his chest and rocked backwards and forwards as if in deep thought. Martin watched him warily.

"There are several points that occur to me and will surely occur to those concerned at the Preparatory Examination, should it come to that! But perhaps you do not need me to enumerate them!"

He glanced across at Martin a moment, then with a bound he was out of his chair.

"I must admit this situation has created something of a problem for me, Dr. Nolan. Although I have my instructions, I feel reluctant to carry them out to the letter. I trust you understand. I propose, therefore, that you make yourself as comfortable here as possible. I have arranged for some excellent books to be brought in, as you will see, and my whiskey too is at your disposal. Your clothing has been brought in but everything else will be handed to you after we dock tomorrow, or perhaps later. Now, if you will pardon me, there is much to be done. This, if you remember, is the last night for many passengers this voyage."

He walked briskly to the door and opened it, then with his hand on the knob he looked back over his shoulder.

"If I were you, Doctor," he said, his jaw thrust aggressively forward, "I'd start praying right now!" And he was gone.

As the door clicked shut, Martin realized he was a prisoner. The actual word had not been mentioned specifically, but it was obvious. He stepped softly forward and tried the door knob gently, but the door remained solidly in position, bolted on the outside.

Could they do this to him? Were they within their rights? he asked himself. Most probably they were, he decided, for the Captain would have radioed for instructions. He groped for the chair and sat down, breathing heavily, for no matter how delicately the allegations had been phrased, the bare truth was that Captain Anderson was holding him captive for the murder of his stupid little wife, now presumed to have been lost overboard. The unfairness of it churned in his brain, but he took a deep breath in an effort to keep calm. He had told Flora that another attack could come at any time, yet he was unable to rest, let alone organize some defence. Presently, with a great sigh, he started to pace slowly around the small cabin.

It was some time before he noticed the orange coloured envelope that was propped against the desk calendar.

He read:

'CONFIDENTIAL AND PERSONAL
MRS. MARTIN NOLAN S.S. GLENCONNOR'

Martin stopped dead in his tracks. This was the radiogram from the Purser's Office! Had the Captain placed it there for him to read?

Martin picked up the envelope and turned it over in his hand. The flap was open. He removed the sheet of paper and as he read the message it contained his blood seemed suddenly to chill to ice. So the Captain, with all his show of hostility, had been kind enough to warn him, to prepare him for more questioning. He felt as if he were being twisted before a distortion mirror. The words snaked up and down before his eyes and when they quietened he read again:

'REQUESTED ANALYSIS AS FOLLOWS: PILL A PAMAQUIN PILL B MEPACRINE BOTH USED IN TREATMENT OF MALARIA SIMULTANEOUS USE NOT RECOMMENDED DUE TO HARMFUL TOXIC REACTIONS SUGGEST DISCONTINUE IMMEDIATELY AND CONSULT DOCTOR — ACME PHARMCO HALIFAX CANADA'

With shaking hands Martin replaced the message and stared before him. So his wife had suspected him of poisoning her! Why else would she have had pills analyzed? He was mystified as to how they had come into Flora's possession, for he had been careful to watch closely that she swallowed them and had checked the numbers remaining in each bottle before replacing them in his medical case. The word 'confidential' disturbed him too. He knew that he would be asked questions because of it and he would be unable to deny that he had possessed the pills mentioned because the half-empty bottles were in the medical case that had been removed from his cabin. The fatal drugs too were in that case. Martin knew then that they would have been useless to him if he had depended on them to kill Flora, for if she was suspicious about the (supposedly) antacid pills and tranquilizers he had given her in Canada, he would never have been able to persuade her that she needed gelatine capsules for added protein as he had planned. He would have had to find some other way of killing her, but one thing was certain — he had not killed her. He would not have pushed Flora through the porthole unless she had been dead and for this he would have had to administer the fatal drugs. The unopened containers, which had been taken from his cabin, would surely be proof enough that he had not used those drugs to kill his wife. He had planned to kill her, of course, but need he tell anyone? If he did, surely the Court would not be able to convict him on the intention to kill when he had changed his mind. But what if they tried to prove that the unopened bottles had been but a blind and that he had secreted another set of fatal drugs somewhere for the purpose and had used those, or that he had found another method of getting rid of his wife? They might even suggest that he had smothered her and pushed her through the porthole during the storm, thus accounting for the telltale wetness on the bedcover which was sure to bother them.

Martin commenced to walk, with measured steps, across the floor. The glorious fact that Flora seemed to have disappeared from his life was more than overshadowed by the dangerous position of chief suspect in which he now found himself. He knew there were several points about his wife's disappearance that would seem strange to legal minds and others. The Preparatory Examination could even develop into a prima facie case in the Cape Town Supreme Court! It might take weeks, possibly months, before the trial came to an end. And in the meantime he would be treated as a common prisoner awaiting trail.

The Captain was right! He had better start praying!

23

THE day the *Glenconnor* was due to arrive, Anthea had been jumpy and bad-tempered and spent hours waiting for a telephone call that had not come. She had been hurt and angry in turn, but as the day wore on she faced the unhappy truth that she had, after all, made the right decision to marry Michael. She had been afraid to tell Martin when he called from London, fearing a coldly furious outburst, but he had not even troubled to telephone on his arrival. He didn't care! That had been a cruel shock to her pride and eventually, like some small dog knocked flying by a passing car, she had crawled away to bed to lick her wounds.

It was 2 a.m. when the telephone rang but it was Tom Meyer, not Martin, who was on the line.

"Anthea," he said. "I have some rather disturbing news. I know it's fearfully late but may I come over?"

"Of course," she said, but her stomach had seemed to take a tumble. She had known instinctively that it concerned Martin and was waiting at the door in gown and slippers when Tom arrived.

"Tell me quickly!" she said softly through clenched teeth. "Is it Martin?"

Tom grasped her shoulders firmly and looked into her eyes, then he nodded slowly.

"He's in grave trouble. Flora is missing."

"Oh, no!" Anthea gasped as she sank into the nearest chair. "What happened?" But even as she asked she knew. Martin had said: 'Flora may let me go — something may happen.' The words had kept running through her head like some recurrent nightmare and now she knew why. She began to shake as though in a state of extreme shock.

"I went to the docks thinking I might be of some help when they arrived," Tom continued, "although Jackson was there with the car. The passengers poured off the ship and through the Customs but there was no sign of the Nolans. I waited around awhile, then went outside to see if

I had missed them, but Jackson was still there and alone. I went back to make inquiries."

Tom sat down opposite Anthea and took her cold hands in his. He began to rub them as though trying to warm them.

"Martin had been asked to remain on board while another thorough search was made of the ship. I asked why, of course, and was told that Flora had not been seen since the evening of the thirteenth, just prior to dinner. There had been a raging storm that day which got progressively worse and eventually reached its peak by 3 a.m. It was suggested that no passenger in his right mind would have thought of going out on deck, so it seemed strange that Flora, a timid soul and not at all well at the time, should have disappeared that night."

Tom shifted position, then continued.

"Whisperings started among the stewards about bad relations between the two, suspicion mounted and finally the Captain ordered Martin taken into custody the following evening."

"He was taken prisoner?"

"Yes."

"Oh, my God!"

Tom continued. "I knew I was not being told the whole story, of course, and was not allowed to see him, but I wangled my way on board and convinced the Captain that Martin had a right to consult his lawyer. A message was sent and Martin sent back word asking me to see his friend and lawyer, Mike Andrews."

"And then?"

"I went first to the parking lot to send Jackson home, then I drove to Mike's office and later his home, but I missed him. He had gone to Paarl on business. I waited around at my club and when I learned Mike was home again I went to see him, late though it was. We chatted for a bit and he decided to see Martin right away. We drove down to the docks but by this time the South African Police had arrived with an official warrant for Martin's arrest and we learned that he had been transferred to the Gaol."

"Did they allow you to see him there?"

"No. But Mike went in to him."

"Did you wait for him?"

"Yes."

"What did he say?"

"Not much really! I suppose it would be confidential but he did mention that Martin would plead 'Not Guilty'."

"NOT guilty?"

Tom looked quickly up at her, then nodded. Anthea pressed his fingers and walked into the kitchenette. She did not trust herself to say anything just then and knew Tom would understand. As she ran the water into the coffee percolator and plugged it in, her thoughts seemed to float round like dandelion seeds in a breeze. She didn't seem able to grasp them, for they would waft tantalizingly out of reach before an idea crystallized.

Unable to still her shaking hands, she clattered the cups and saucers on the tray and stood waiting for the coffee to finish percolating. She needed a few moments to be alone to absorb the grim tidings.

Her first reaction had been stark horror and she was disgusted with herself. Someone in love would surely rush into the arms of her loved one, but not level-headed Anthea Curtis! Oh no! Suddenly Anthea hated herself. She had been accused in the past of being calculating and she had been annoyed, but now she was not so sure they had been wrong. She was thinking of herself at a time like this — putting her own comfort and convenience before Martin's need. She had thought she loved him, but had she ever been in love with him? Was it perhaps the good-looking, successful surgeon figure that had fascinated her? She did not know. All that seemed real at the present time was her revulsion at the thought of being close to him. In her eyes he was a murderer, whether convicted or not, and no woman in any sense of delicacy could bear to be touched by hands that had killed, coldly and deliberately.

Maybe she would be forgiven for not going to him now, but forgiven by whom? The busy little housewife with ears pressed to the radio for news of this latest excitement? By Martin? No — he would never forgive her, she knew. He might even hate her when he learned that she was to marry Michael, yet she had tried to tell him when he telephoned from London and he too had tried to tell her that he would be free!

She stared blindly at the brown liquid bubbling up into the lid of the coffee pot and when it subsided finally, she poured the coffee into the cups, spilling some in her efforts. She mopped hastily around and called to Tom.

"Please carry the tray for me. I'm sure to drop it!"

He was beside her in an instant and soon they were solemnly looking at each other above their steaming cups.

"What are we going to do?" whispered Anthea.

"Stand solidly behind him, I suppose! Show him that he has two friends at least that he can rely upon."

Anthea shook her head slowly from side to side.

"I can't," she said simply. "For one thing it would look bad and perhaps start rumours of another woman in the case. For another, I think it will be kinder in the end to let him know where he stands with me, and that is not solidly behind him, but as far away as I can get — in Australia!"

She saw Tom frown suddenly and she

smiled but her lips were quivering.

"You think I'm the most despicable bitch, don't you? You can't understand how anyone can rat on a pal like this! Dear Tom! You are so naive. I hate to disillusion you but the fact is that I'm getting married in a couple of weeks. I shall shake the dust of this unpleasant business from my newest shoes and never even think of it again!"

Tom's eyes were wide with amazement and suddenly Anthea burst into sobs. The coffee spilled down the front of her gown and went on spilling. Tom reached over and took the cup from her.

"You don't really mean that and you know it," he said kindly but Anthea shook her head vehemently.

"I do mean it! I don't want to be around when he finds out he killed Flora so as to be able to marry me and I'm not even staying for the trial!"

Tom gasped. "Is that what you think, Anthea? That Martin killed Flora to marry you?"

"Yes. He almost admitted as much, but I was too blind to realize it at the time."

They stared at each other.

"I couldn't let him touch me now — I don't even want to see him! Can you understand that?"

Her eyes were imploring and Tom shifted uncomfortably in his chair.

"You realize we're convicting him in our minds of a crime he may not have committed?"

Anthea nodded.

"Even if he were acquitted it would make no difference. I'm through! I notice you said 'we.' Are you with me in this?"

Tom studied the pattern on the carpet as if counting the squares, then he sat back and let his eyes come to rest on Anthea.

"I never meant to tell anyone," he said, his voice hardly more than a whisper, as though he sought to excuse his actions, not to Anthea but to himself. Then he continued.

"For many years I've felt there was something strange about Martin. He seemed to be playing a game of some sort, but whether to bluff me or to fool himself I never could decide. Now, I think it was, perhaps, part of a well thought out plan."

It was Anthea's turn to look surprised.

"Yes," Tom went on. "I believe he wanted people to think Flora was an alcoholic but he never sent her for any positive treatment. My hunch is that she didn't need any. She drank — that's for sure — but not the way he wanted it to look. He was always dropping hints, letting it be known she was having one of her 'spells,' but I saw her picking flowers and reading happily in the summerhouse on two different occasions when she was supposed to be under the influence."

"You said nothing?"

"No. What could I say?"

"Of course! What could anyone?"

Tom drained the remainder of his coffee and sat forward as if choosing his words with care. Anthea waited.

"Then," Tom continued, "after the Annual Ball, when Martin took ill, I went to see him. When I went into his bathroom to wash my hands I noticed quite a few bottles of pills and medicines in the cabinet, yet he had remarked rather pointedly only moments before that he kept no drugs around the house ever, insinuating that Flora might be tempted to take her own life, I suppose. Among these bottles two stood out clearly, one marked pamaquin and the other mepacrine."

He stopped and Anthea saw he was waiting for some reaction from her.

"I don't follow," she said. "Did someone there have malaria?"

Tom looked serious. "That's just the point! Neither Martin nor Flora had ever been further north in Africa than Johannesburg — in fact I don't think Flora ever left Cape Town and the vicinity. I kept thinking about this. I felt there was something I should remember about those two drugs. After Martin left to join Flora in Edmonton, I went to the house and asked Jackson if I might look in his master's bathroom for some pills that I needed. He let me in, of course, and stood waiting while I went through the supply. It did not take me more than a few seconds to realize the two bottles had gone. I thanked Jackson and said I would have to get what I needed at the hospital, and went on my way."

"But what does it mean?"

Tom leaned closer. "Don't you remember your pharmacology?"

Anthea looked questioningly at him.

Tom continued. "I checked with Sapieka's *Actions and Uses of Drugs* and there it was! Something like 'simultaneous administration of mepacrine and pamaquin appears to aggravate the toxicity of each'."

"And the toxic effects?"

"I forget but I know there were epigastric pain, mental derangement, organic disturbance of the nervous system, hepatitis, liver necrosis, etc., etc."

"And you think he was poisoning her slowly with these?"

"Maybe not! As you know, massive doses would have been required and they might have proved fatal. I think he was trying to frighten her into the belief that she had cancer, or something of the sort, and hoping she might take her own life. If she didn't, maybe he decided to do it for her. He might even have persuaded her that he was doing her a great favour."

"I don't want to believe it," Anthea

said softly, "yet I know that every word could be true and possibly is! What do we do now?"

"God! I don't know!" Tom said, his voice cracking with emotion. "I'm praying that no one calls me to give evidence! He thinks I'm his friend!"

The words seemed wrung from Tom like a soul in torment.

★ ★ ★

After Tom left her, sleep had been impossible and eventually Anthea bathed and dressed as though in a dream. She ate toast and drank tea and juice without conscious thought and drove to the hospital. All day she moved mechanically through her duties, numb in mind and body as though she had been emptied of all feeling. She felt unable to register emotion or think clearly, and by the end of her working day she felt she had become like a carved wooden statue.

"Argee! Argee! Read all about it!" came the raucous cries of the Cape Coloured newsboys as they held out folded copies of the evening newspaper.

Anthea fumbled hastily for coins, took the *Cape Argus* with trembling hands and turned to the front page. Her body chilled in horror. It was all there — splashed in lurid detail — even to the ghastly picture of Martin taken many years ago! All around her a bustling mob of after-five office workers surged along Adderley Street in their rush for homeward-bound trains and buses, but Anthea stood spellbound. So it was true! Flora really had disappeared at sea and Martin was being charged with murder!

Suddenly she felt ill. She folded the newspaper, tucked it under her arm and slowly made her way to the parking lot. She knew she would have to summon all her strength to get through the evening with her usual grace.

As she slid behind the wheel of her Volkswagen and began to move ant-like into the stream of traffic heading towards the Gardens and the Mount Nelson Hotel, where she was to have dinner with an old friend, she wished she had been able to wriggle out of the engagement. Ordinarily this would have been an evening to look forward to, but now she dreaded it and prayed silently that there would be no mention of the current topic of conversation — the Nolan Affair!

24

AT the start of the Preparatory Examination Martin's attitude had been almost one of annoyance. As he watched the Magistrate dispassionately taking down the evidence, he had the feeling that he was a spectator at a charade, and a slightly unpleasant one at that. He could not relate his position to that of the man in the dock. After all, he knew he had not killed anyone, so what was he doing watching the process of justice in a matter which could not possibly concern him?

By the end of the day the force of the proceedings had started to sink in and, with a progressive chill, the awful realization of his predicament enveloped him. When the Magistrate, suddenly invading Martin's haphazard but now anxious thoughts, asked him in a stern, but remote and level tone of voice whether he, Martin Nolan, had anything to say and that he, the accused,

Martin Nolan, must realize that he was not obliged to say anything but that if he did whatever he said would be taken down in writing and used as evidence against him at his trial, then Martin knew that it was he, and no one else but he, who was going to be tried for murder.

He cleared his voice and opened his mouth, but no words came. He tried again and then mercifully, Mike Andrews stood up and said "Your Worship, we reserve our defence."

This seemed to satisfy the proceedings for the Magistrate merely kept on writing and nothing more was said.

★ ★ ★

After Martin had been committed to the Supreme Court for trial, Mike Andrews had suggested that Bertram Ogilvie should be briefed. Martin had been relieved at the choice. He knew Ogilvie to be a florid, flamboyant figure of a man with a peppery temper to match, a forbidding eye, and the curious habit of pivoting on the tips of his toes, and had felt that he had found someone who would not flinch under fire.

Ogilvie, when approached, had been bouncing with good humour and 'delighted to have the honour,' as he put it, of defending Martin, but gradually Martin had watched this good humour change, almost imperceptively at first, to one of slight concern and then abruptly to consternation.

"I don't understand you!" the man had boomed. "You have nothing to gain by not telling me the whole truth. I'm here to help you! In any case, half truths and lies will have only one effect — to discredit your word to a jury! Now — I want to hear EXACTLY what happened and don't keep saying 'I didn't kill her' like some broken talking doll! We shall get nowhere this way!"

He had calmed down, then, almost deliberately disciplining his temper and suggested that they should start again — with the facts!

"FACTS, mind you!" he had bellowed suddenly, and Martin, like the smashed talking doll he had been accused of becoming, had repeated over and over again the same answers.

"Yes. My wife and I had not been happy together. It was, unfortunately, well known. No, neither Flora nor I had ever had malaria. Yes, I took the pills with me to Canada. I always carried an assortment in my travelling case. Yes, my wife went by ship and I followed some time later by air. No, my wife was not given anything for malaria when she left me. Only I took those particular pills. I thought we might need them on our trip."

Ogilvie raised his hands and dropped them down again in a gesture of despair.

"I don't believe it!" he declared, as if to himself. Then, raising his voice and speaking clearly he began again.

"Doctor! For a man of your intelligence your behaviour is remarkably juvenile and I fail to understand why. I am no fool and neither will be the Judge, I'm sure, so for the last time let me advise you that I am interested only in the truth from you. What I choose to do with that information and how I present it must be my own concern. I do not intend to waste my valuable time unless you understand this clearly."

Martin flushed. He licked his dry lips and swallowed, then the words came. "I wanted to give them to my wife."

"Those were the pills your daughter saw you give to your wife on several occasions?"

"Yes."

"You gave your wife mepacrine and pamaquin together with bicarbonate of soda while in Canada?"

"I did."

"But why? You say neither of you had ever suffered from malaria."

"I knew they would make her ill. I wanted her to think she had jaundice."

"Now we are getting somewhere!" Ogilvie shouted, banging his fist on the table. Then calmly — "Why?"

"I wanted her to think she was suffering from a diseased liver, perhaps cancer."

"But she had no such diseased liver?"

"I don't know. She may have! She drank a good deal."

"But you hoped she and everyone else

would think she had?"

"Yes."

"Why?"

Martin did not answer but his eyes blazed in sudden anger.

Ogilvie watched him closely, then he spoke again.

"Doctor, it may help you to answer if I tell you that I know. I want to hear it from you!" His voice was soft yet strangely menacing.

Martin swallowed again. "So that if I killed her it would look like suicide. But I didn't . . . "

Bertram Ogilvie raised his hand to silence him. "You have made that clear," he said decisively. "So you proposed to kill her. Is that why you carried two bottles of deadly drugs — one of sodium cyanide and one of potassium bisulphate — all the way to Canada and back again?"

"Yes, but I didn't use them. I changed my mind."

"And why did you change your mind?"

"I took ill: a slight heart attack. My wife was extremely kind. I knew I could not go through with it."

"Because you were ill or because your wife had been kind?"

"A little of each perhaps."

Ogilvie sat back.

"Now, Doctor," he said, spinning his pen quickly between his thumb and forefinger as he looked at the notes before him, "to return to the idea of suicide. You said that if you killed your wife you hoped it would look like suicide. Was your wife the type of woman who would be able to destroy herself — pull a trigger, slash her wrist, climb overboard?"

Martin put a trembling hand to his head and smoothed back his already smooth hair. Then he answered.

"No."

"Then what do you believe actually happened after she left you?"

"I don't know. I only wish I did! All I can think is that she may, perhaps, have been washed overboard accidentally."

"So you think she may have gone out in that dreadful storm?"

"Maybe."

"Well — one guess is as good as another at this point! Now — how did you propose to kill your wife?"

"I planned to remove the gelatine from a capsule and replace it with the two drugs I had brought. This would have been done just prior to giving them to her, of course. I should have had to be extremely cautious — make certain that I kept one drug to one side and the other drug to the other side. But I decided against it, as I told you. I never opened the bottles."

"Doctor," said Ogilvie, "*I* believe you but the point is, who else will?"

They looked at each other, then Ogilvie went on.

"The damp bedcover. You say the porthole blew open during the night?"

"Yes. I had to climb out of bed to close it."

"Had it ever done that before?"

"Not that I know of, but there was a ferocious wind blowing."

"You would not have opened the porthole to push your wife's body through?"

"No, no! I've told you! I didn't kill her! The porthole blew open because of the wind."

Ogilvie sat forward, his eyes shrinking

to pinpoints as he looked into Martin's face.

"We have here a situation in which the accused administers certain pills to his wife, leading her to believe she is taking antacids and a tranquilizer. These pills, taken together, are known to cause toxic symptoms and the accused hopes his wife will believe she has cancer of the liver, while others will see she looks ill, so that when she is killed — by an ingenious method of substituting lethal drugs for the gelatine in a capsule — it will look like suicide, the wife supposedly preferring death by her own hand to that of the presumed cancer. The accused, having set up this most elaborate scheme, changes his mind and decides not to kill her after all because she was kind to him when he became ill? Then, rather too conveniently I fear, the wife ventures out on deck in a storm and is accidentally washed overboard!"

Martin lowered his lids, shutting a mental door between them, as the man persisted.

"We have also the night steward's report of a scene. The report states clearly that you had tried to choke her! Now — what do you have to say to that?"

"I lost my head! I never had any intention of choking her."

"Well — could she later have developed strange symptoms and died from natural causes? In a panic, perhaps you got rid of the body through the porthole?"

Martin placed his head in his hands.

"So you, too, don't really believe me! I've told you! I didn't kill her! She must have been washed overboard."

"Over the high ship's rail?"

Martin shook his head in despair. "I don't know! I don't know anything except that I planned to kill but did not!"

"I see."

For a while there was silence, then Bertram Ogilvie cleared his throat.

"Fortunately or unfortunately — depending on which way you look at it — there is no body. It will be difficult to prove she was killed as it will be to prove that she died by her own hand or was accidentally lost at sea. The fact that you may be innocent of her death is of little account. What I need — what I must have — is proof that she killed herself or was lost at sea, otherwise the whole defence may be useless. I'm not sure I'll be able to convince anyone of your innocence. I might just conceivably have pulled it off if it had not been for the diary."

Martin looked up, his face a picture of astonishment, as though caught by a flash bulb and recorded on photographic paper.

"Yes. You were not aware that your wife had kept a diary?"

"No!" The word was a whisper as Martin stared in horror and disbelief at his Counsel, flipping now through papers in his briefcase.

"The last entry was 7 a.m. on the morning of the 13th of June, while watching over you," Ogilvie continued.

He removed a few sheets for which he had been searching and Martin saw they were photocopies of pages from Flora's diary.

She had written some entries in pencil and some with a ballpoint pen that apparently needed a refill for the ink flow had been erratic. Martin's eyes followed each word as his Counsel read aloud:

"But maybe Martin's attack will change the course of my life. He could die before he has time to kill me. I should be free! Dear God! I don't dare think about it! But if he gets over this, what then? I have forgotten that he told me once I would have to pay for what I had done to him, and I've never known him to change his mind . . ."

Ogilvie sat back to look searchingly at his client, obviously waiting for some word, but Martin could only continue to stare at him, his lips working but uttering no sound. The next moment, with a low moan, he put his head in his hands and slumped forward with his head on the desk.

So Flora had known he was waiting to kill her, just as she had known that he was giving her pills that were not meant to cure. She had written in a diary, in black and white, for the whole world to read! Nothing could save him, yet he was innocent. He had not killed his wife, he had only planned to do so. There was a world of difference between the two, but who would believe him? Even his own Counsel for the Defence believed him guilty. He would be convicted of murdering Flora and sentenced — to death, ten years, twenty years, or life — what would it matter now? All because he had fallen in love with a young, vivacious, tantalizingly beautiful woman who had not even cared for him enough to stay for his trial, to lend her presence, let alone support, in his time of need. Certainly no one would believe him. Why should they if his own daughter, the greatest love of his life, his greatest gift, had turned her back on him and condemned him by her very absence?

25

SEVERAL weeks later the Nolan Trial commenced at the Cape Town Supreme Court. A watery sun peeped hesitantly through the glass panes of the courtroom. The atmosphere was chilly and the air stale.

Inconspicuous in the upstairs gallery sat Tom, looking around him and wriggling his toes inside his shoes as his chilblains itched. He wished he had not felt in duty bound to attend. His thoughts were sad, as though a great load of past memories clung tenaciously to his back to bow him down.

He and Martin had been friends — or almost friends — for far more years than he liked to remember and he knew that, no matter what the outcome of this trial that was about to begin, their friendship was finally over, thrown into the wastepaper basket like some discarded valentine. He could not hope to understand what had happened to Martin, a man who appeared to have everything — an above average intelligence, wealth, and good looks. He gave a deep sigh and settled back.

As Tom looked around he made a mental note of those present and those who, in his opinion, should have been present. Among the former he was most surprised to see Dr. Pennington, old Godfrey Maxmillian himself, looking as doddery as ever but still as sharp as a prickly pear thorn, taking a keen interest, apparently, in a matter that concerned one of 'his boys.'

Of those whom Tom considered conspicuous by their absence were Anthea and Beth. He felt there was some excuse for Anthea not to have remained in South Africa for the trial, for by being in Court she might have drawn people's attention to the fact that there had been an affair of some sort going on, but Beth he could not forgive.

In the beginning he felt sure Beth would fly over immediately she heard of her mother's presumed death and her father's possible part in it, to lend her support, if nothing else, but there had been just silence, a strange and utter silence that had bewildered him. He had known and loved her from the day she was born and, being a bachelor, had enjoyed his role of 'adopted uncle' over the years. He did not understand and decided to put in an overseas call to her, at some phenomenally high cost to himself too, to make sure she understood the predicament in which her father found himself and to suggest that she might appear in time for the trial.

Beth had answered the telephone herself, as Tom had hoped, Edmonton time being then just after midnight.

"Hello! Uncle Tom! How good to hear from you!" she said, immediately wide awake and obviously delighted to hear his voice. But the next moment she had closed up like a shellfish, her hard exterior apparently impervious to his probing. At last she spoke, her voice packed with venom.

"Yes, I understand, Uncle Tom! Perfectly! My mother is dead they tell me, and my father is on trial for having killed her. What makes you think I could be of any possible help in a situation like that?"

Tom had been flabbergasted.

"But Beth," he said, "your father needs you. You are all he has left in the whole world!"

"Except his lady friend!" she snapped. So she knew!

"No," said Tom. "There is no girl friend."

"You mean she has deserted the sinking ship?"

Tom did not know how to answer. He ignored the question and instead repeated himself.

"My dear, don't you realize? You are all your father has and he is not well. Won't you please come to him?"

There was a mirthless laugh through the earpiece. "Uncle Tom! If my father is convicted it will be, most probably, what he deserves. If he is set free it will make no difference to me. I don't want to see him again."

"Child! What are you saying?" he had gasped. "Are you punishing him before you know if he is guilty?"

"Exactly that! And you can tell him so from me if you wish. I shall never forgive him, ever, for the years of cruel treatment of my mother who loved him and depended entirely upon him. I can't forgive myself either for allowing it, but I did not understand. That's my only excuse. I've not even mentioned Mother's possible murder, did you notice, Uncle Tom? Dad may have to answer for that too, I don't know. Let the Court decide. I am pronouncing him guilty for what he did to my mother these long years."

Tom had been too stupefied to try to reason with her. Softly he replaced the receiver, not quite believing what he had heard. What could have happened in Canada? Beth and Martin had been so close that he had even worried that the situation was becoming unhealthy. This sudden turn-about was a shock for which he was totally unprepared.

Now Tom sat back, focusing his attention on the prisoner who was being brought into the courtroom. He had not seen Martin for several weeks and was shocked to see how shaken and pale he had become. It seemed almost as if he had shrunk in size. His suit hung unpressed from his frame that had lost its proud set of the head and ramrod back, but what disturbed Tom Meyer most was the beaten dog look that had replaced the arrogance in Martin's eyes.

"Martin Nolan, you stand charged upon this indictment with murder in that on the thirteenth day of June, 1972, and on the high seas on the steamship *Glenconnor* you did wilfully murder your lawful wife, Flora Elizabeth Nolan. How do you plead to that charge, guilty or not guilty?"

"Not guilty."

The words were barely audible.

The jury were empanelled and sworn. The Prosecutor shuffled papers and cleared his throat preparatory to presenting his case, but Tom could bear no more. He slid quietly from the hard wooden bench and made his escape. He could see Martin was not even prepared to put up a strong resistance. He was beaten before he had begun!

26

AS the trial dragged on, Martin looked dully around the courtroom, almost bored by the proceedings. Each day seemed to bring a fresh flock of inquisitive faces, each with the same sharp eyes waiting to pounce on a new tidbit. He was weary of looking at them. On some days the sun shone and on others it was overcast, but every day was cold and damp. He seemed now to have a permanent ache in his chest, and as each morning dawned he registered a mild surprise that he was still alive.

Three words — insinuation, supposition, and circumstantial — were repeated time and again by Bertram Ogilvie as he asserted that the entire case against his client rested on a flimsy foundation indeed. Martin's denials seemed to stack up feebly in the face of the growing mountain of circumstantial evidence, motive, and coincidence building up slowly but surely against him.

After admitting that he gave his wife pills to induce toxic reactions, it seemed of little account to stress that the bottle of gelatine capsules and the bottles of sodium cyanide and potassium bisulphate had remained unopened. Even if he had changed his mind (as he claimed) about poisoning his wife by introducing the two fatal drugs in one of the capsules, it was argued that the intention to kill was there. It was suggested that Martin could have used another method — one that was not planned perhaps, but which was used when an opportunity presented itself. However, no one knew for sure how Mrs. Nolan had died or even if she had died at all!

It was this point that had the members of the jury worried.

Everything pointed clearly to Martin's guilt; he had even admitted having in his possession certain deadly drugs and of administering others that were potentially harmful. He had admitted that he had planned to kill his wife, but with no body how could one be completely sure that she was dead? The possibilities could not be overlooked too that she might have been lost accidentally during the storm or that she had found the necessary courage to take her own life, though lack of a suicide note seemed to rule out the latter.

It was again mentioned that Martin had suffered a heart attack and that his wife had looked after him with devotion, causing him to change his mind about killing her. To back this up there was the fact that no attempt had been made by him to hide any of the possibly damning evidence. There had been no signs of a struggle and no incriminating marks on the porthole, but there had been a most damaging entry in Flora's diary.

The pendulum swung one way and then another with the introduction of each new piece of evidence brought forward and torn to shreds by the sharp tongues of the two barristers and at the close of the third day the end was still nowhere in sight. The Court again adjourned.

★ ★ ★

Molly Mears, blinded by a sudden rush of tears that threatened to fall, fumbled in her handbag for a handkerchief as she stepped out of the Supreme Court Building into the late afternoon sunlight. Her low-heeled, black shoes, polished to a high gloss, looked neat but old-fashioned, her full-length coat hung loosely with no belt to emphasize her full corsetted figure. One might have thought her a nun, having shed the severe habit of an order yet unable to relinquish entirely the forbidding, unimaginative mode of dress.

She could scarcely believe what was happening. That Dr. Nolan, her Dr. Nolan, was on trial for murdering his wife was simply monstrous! Someone must help him before it was too late! The State Prosecutor was out to trip him up! He'd have the Doctor confessing for the sake of peace and then what? It made her ill to think about it.

Finding her handkerchief at last, she blew her nose vigorously and walked across the street to a coffee shop for a light supper.

As she sat down at a round table beside the window, her handbag flew open and the contents spilled in all directions.

"Oh, how clumsy of me!" she mumbled, bending down to gather everything together and smiling her thanks to the well-built, rather stocky man who fell to his knees to grope under the table for her.

When order was restored, she realized that he had not resumed his seat but was standing behind the chair opposite to her, his hand resting lightly on the back. He smiled charmingly.

"Would you mind if I joined you?" he asked in a deep voice with the hint of a Scots accent. "I noticed you in Court today. Perhaps you would have supper with me?"

Miss Mears nodded a surprised assent. This was the nicest thing that had happened to her for some time, she thought, to have a nice-looking robust young man (no, not so young, she corrected mentally) take an interest in her and she wondered why.

"Forgive me," he said, "but I noticed you were upset. I wondered if you were related to Dr. or Mrs. Nolan."

"Dear me, no!" Miss Mears said, her shiny nose wrinkling at the idea. "I am Dr. Nolan's secretary — or perhaps I should have said WAS!"

She patted the plump folds on her wrists in agitation.

"He has given up his practice then?"

"Yes. It has been taken over by a much younger man. I did not feel I wanted to stay. There were too many memories! I showed the new girl the ropes for a while and now I am taking a holiday!"

"A holiday? Sitting in Court every day?"

He smiled again and Miss Mears smiled too, though she glanced down feeling like a child caught out.

"Dr. Nolan is very dear to me," she said by way of explanation. "I have lived alone since my parents died many years ago. I had only my work to look forward to, and I found it most rewarding. I simply idolized Dr. Nolan, but he was a busy man."

Suddenly the tears again welled up and threatened to fall. As she brushed them angrily away, she saw the kindness in her companion's eyes and knew that he had guessed that the tears were not altogether on account of Dr. Nolan's plight.

"Do you think the doctor will be convicted?"

Molly's eyes rested solemnly on his for some moments before she answered.

"I am afraid so, but that does not mean that I believe him guilty. He is a fine man and he must have had a sad life. I don't blame him for wanting to kill his wife, but I don't think he did."

"You don't blame him for wanting to kill his wife?" His voice sounded shocked, and Molly Mears looked again into his eyes.

"I don't know why I am talking to you like this," she said softly. "You have not told me who you are! If I find out you are a reporter, I shall be very angry!"

She set her mouth in a stubborn line and sat bolt upright in her chair, but when she was treated to another of his charming smiles and a shake of the head, she melted again.

"So you are not a reporter?"

"No. I live in the city but spend a good deal of time away. When I arrived back yesterday I was shocked to see the headlines in the newspapers. I knew Mrs. Nolan only slightly but I decided to attend Court today."

"You are then what one would call an 'interested spectator'?"

"That is right. I have a few days to myself with nothing much to do to fill the time."

Molly Mears nodded understandingly, attended to the serious business of choosing her meal as the waiter approached to take their orders, and then continued.

"A murder trial seems to attract many people who have nothing better to do, doesn't it? I have seen very few so-called friends of the doctor — and not even his daughter — yet every day the courtroom was full."

Jock McPherson looked across at her.

"Was he a popular man?" he asked.

"No. He was arrogant, self-assured and smarter than many, if not all, of his colleagues so, of course, he was not popular. He was an unerringly correct diagnostician and his surgery, they tell me, was deftly and speedily done, but he lacked warmth. Patients and nurses alike walked in fear of a rebuke and even I was a little afraid of him, though not any more!"

Self-consciously she wiped away a falling tear.

"Doctor preferred to be left alone, but I often thought he should have had some outside interests or hobbies to fall back upon. It must have been soul-destroying to find his wife so often imbibing too freely when he arrived home. He hated any abuse of liquor and despised anyone who indulged. I can well understand how hatred could have set in, so that finally he wanted to put an end to her."

"Was there another woman do you think?"

"I heard so. I admit I am surprised that not a whisper has come out in the courtroom. It is just as well, or that would have been but one more black mark against him."

"Do you think he would have wanted to murder his wife because of this other woman?" he asked.

"Maybe. I don't really know. I only know that I believe him when he declares he did not murder her."

"You do?"

"Yes. Long ago I suspected the doctor might try to get rid of her. He had encircled the 13th of June on his desk calendar with a black felt pen."

Jock looked inquiringly at her, his mouth full of beef sandwich.

"Yes," Molly continued. "He was always a most methodical and orderly person. He recorded everything of importance at the office. I arranged the overseas trips for both the doctor and his wife and I knew there was nothing of any significance planned for the 13th of June. After Dr. Nolan left for Edmonton I gave this matter a great deal of thought. If he had used an ordinary ball point pen I should not have worried, but I knew that to him that deep black felt circle meant something extraordinarily serious."

She smiled across at Jock, then took a few sips of her tea before continuing.

"You must understand that I worked for the doctor for many years," she added. "Very often I found I was able to anticipate what was required. I knew what he was thinking! When I heard that Mrs. Nolan had disappeared on that day I was not really surprised. I felt certain that he had at last put an end to his misery with her, but when I learned the details I knew that such a fastidious, methodical and brilliant man would never leave such telltale and damning evidence around for everyone to see. I am sure that he planned to kill her but did not go through with it, as he claims."

Jock swallowed his mouthful in a gulp. "Do you think they will convict him even though he may be innocent?"

"I'm afraid so, but until there is proof that he actually killed or even proof that she is dead, he still has a chance, though in the end there may be little difference."

She sighed. "I don't know much about the law," she went on, "but whether the doctor is acquitted or given a stiff sentence, his career and his health have taken a severe beating. They may never recover!"

Jock nodded slowly. "And if they give him the death sentence?"

"IF they can, of course! I think the shock may kill him, but perhaps that would be the most merciful thing."

"I don't think he'd get more than ten or twenty years, do you?"

"Ten or twenty years!" Molly Mears's voice was shrill with indignation.

"Well, would that not be fair? Can you imagine what it must have been like for his wife to be waiting day after day, maybe even year after year, for the fateful day when he would finally decide to do away with her?"

"Yes," Molly answered, her voice low. "It must have been terrifying, but perhaps she deserved it?"

There was a sudden silence, then she added, "You say you knew her only slightly?"

"Yes, for just a short while."

They looked at each other but Jock's gaze did not flinch.

"Will you be in Court tomorrow," Molly asked at last.

"No, I don't think so. I shall have to read the verdict in the papers."

"Of course! There are the papers, but I shall come again, every day if necessary, until this thing is settled. I have a feeling that Dr. Nolan will be glad to see me then. Maybe he will even realize that I am his friend."

She rose, a sad smile twisting her prim

mouth, and nodded toward Jock.

"It was nice meeting you," she said, "and thank you for a delicious supper."

Jock too had risen. "It was my pleasure," he said as Miss Mears picked up her bag and moved heavily across the floor of the coffee shop, out into the darkening winter evening.

"Such a charming man," she murmured, "but he did not want me to know his name. I wonder why."

27

TWO young boys raced each other along the deserted beach at Bloubergstrand, their bare feet flipping the white sea sand behind them in the wind. Jock McPherson looked after them and laughed as he collapsed beside a jagged boulder and rolled over to the lee side.

"I can't keep up with the young devils anymore," he remarked to his wife. "I'm getting really old!"

She looked lovingly across at him, then picked up a bit of seaweed and ran it along the beach making soft patterns.

"Aren't we all?" she said softly.

Carefully she moved some of the dry sand to one side and began to draw in the slightly damp sand underneath.

After some while he said, "What are you doing?"

"I'm drawing you."

He laughed. "Surely I don't look like that?"

"Yes," she said firmly. "A cross between old Father Neptune and King Kong!"

He roared at that, got to his feet and sauntered over to view the artistry at close quarters.

"You horror!" he chuckled, playfully pushing her over and trickling a handful of sand and crushed shells inside her sweater. It was her turn to yell. Then Jock grew serious. He dropped down beside her, drew her gently into his arms and held her close, his chin nestling in her fair curls.

"My darling," he said, his voice breaking with emotion, "I love you so much!"

After a while she drew away from him and looked into his eyes, deeply and with understanding. "Something has happened, hasn't it Jock? Can you tell me about it?"

"No — not yet. Maybe one day! But because of it I realise how much you mean to me — and the boys too. Suddenly I can't bear the thought of going back to sea."

"My dear! And your ship? What about

her — your first love?"

"I don't know. Perhaps she is, after all, my second love."

She looked steadily at him, then raised his hand to her cheek. "It must have been something pretty devastating!"

He smiled but his eyes were sad. "Yes, in a way it was."

"And was it something to do with your secret little excursion into town yesterday?"

Jock ruffled her hair lovingly, then dropped a quick kiss in the nape of he neck. "However did you guess?"

"Because I love you," she said simply and broke away from him. "Now I'll race you to the boys."

She was up and off down the beach but Jock remained as she had left him, resting on one elbow, his feet half buried in the sand. He looked with tender eyes at the slim figure running lithely along the shore, the small waves lapping up as if to lick her bare toes. Further along the beach the boys were having a tug-of-war with a long rope of seaweed, the muscles in their sunburnt legs bulging with iron strength. Across the blue water of the bay lay the city of Cape Town with its white table cloth of cloud spread over the flat top of the mountain.

Jock sighed with a deep contentment. There was nothing more at that moment that he needed, nothing he could possibly wish for, but what of Flora? What agonies must she have endured knowing not only that her husband did not love her, but that he was waiting to see her die! Jock's mouth set in a grim line.

Presently he put his hand inside the breast pocket of his squall jacket and drew out a large envelope containing several sheets of notepaper bearing the crest of the *S.S. Glenconnor*. He looked around to make sure he was alone, then he leaned his back against a smooth rock and proceeded once again to read through Flora's letter that he had received the previous day, with other mail, at the shipping company. It had been addressed to the Cape Town office, clearly marked 'To await arrival,' yet by some quirk of fate or plain inefficiency, it had followed him half way around the globe to Montreal and back. He did not like this sort of message from the grave — it sent cold prickles up and down his spine — but he knew he must read it, again and again, until he understood what it was that he had to do.

'Dearest Jock,' he read,
'It seems strange to be sitting here in this old-fashioned chair in the writing room and writing to you after all these long weeks. I had promised myself it was something I would never do, yet here I am, not having the strength to deny myself one last opportunity of "talking" to you. This is a rather one-sided conversation, but it will have to serve for we shall not meet again. I shall not be able to hear your voice, ever, saying "Flora my dear" the way you used to when we were alone. I find that a sombre thought and it chills me.

My visit to my daughter and wee Jamie was more successful than I had dreamed it could be. Arthur, understanding perhaps, kept busy so that we three were alone together a good deal. The baby is the most beautiful boy and of course twined himself around my heartstrings at once. Beth and I seemed, for the first time ever, to understand each other and I am more than grateful for that interlude. It meant much to me, as you knew it would.

My husband arrived on schedule and disaster struck. I did not seem able to talk to him, or to anyone, and suddenly felt very ill. I thought my nerves were playing up now that he was back with me, just watching and waiting, and when he gave me pills to take — the usual procedure — I saw immediately that they were different. Though naturally apprehensive, I took them and after several days discovered that I was jaundiced. It occured to me that Martin had given me special pills for a reason. He was either poisoning me slowly or he wanted me (and perhaps others) to think I was suffering from liver trouble. I stopped taking them but managed to hide two of the pills which I sent later for analysis in Halifax on my way home. The report is due shortly, but what the pills contain no longer matters, to me or to anyone.

Still nauseated from time to time and ever on the alert, I left Edmonton on schedule, met Martin in England and we began our voyage home. This has been a complete nightmare!

Bad feeling between us flared up finally when Martin, who had been behaving oddly, lost his temper and almost choked me. For one ghastly instant I thought my time had come but I should have realized, as I do now, that strangling is not his style! I am convinced that he had taken his hands from around my neck before I pressed the buzzer to summon the steward.

However, this affair depressed me dreadfully and I was confused. I did not really want to die, yet why should I want to live? I asked myself this question time and time again, but did not seem able to find an answer.

Soon afterwards Martin took ill — a heart attack. I was terrified that he would die. I'd never been close to death and was afraid, at first, even to sleep. But then it occured to me that if Martin died I should be free, providing of course that the pills he had given me were not some slow-acting poison. I decided that the first thing to do was to check my health.

The ships's doctor gave me a thorough examination while Martin slept and he asked me to call later for the results of certain tests. I had given a false name so that Martin should not discover what I had done. Fortunately I was not missed. Martin awoke soon after I returned and seemed much better and I was back where I had been before his attack — just waiting for the axe.

Then, like a slap across the mouth, Martin intimated that he had planned to kill me but that he could not go through with it. I was stupefied, as you can imagine. He asked me, too, to leave him so that Anthea would know when the ship docked that our marriage was over.

Horrified and hurt in turn I left the cabin, vowing never to see Martin again. I could not stop thinking about what he had said and for some time must have wandered aimlessly around. At last I awoke to the realization that

I was expected at the doctor's office for the test results. Stumbling my way across, feeling dreadfully ill, I crowned it all by having a dizzy spell in the doctor's room!

To get to the point — I never should have guessed, nor you my darling, the reason for a good deal of the intermittent nausea and vomiting and even my fainting spell today. A Brevindex test performed on a specimen of my urine was positive! The doctor told me that, without any possible doubt, I was pregnant. You will know what this means, Jock. It is our child that I am carrying — our baby — probably not much bigger than a pea at this stage, but our very own. I have always adored children and the tragedy is that now, after all these years, and at the mellow age of forty, there seems no way that I can bring him into the world.

Martin's words have been running through my head ever since he spoke to me. I have kept repeating them over and over again as though I did not quite understand them. "I want you to leave me. I want you to leave me!" Only now that I am writing to you do I understand what I must do and what Martin, perhaps, meant me to do. (Am I being fanciful as you once told me? I do not know. All that is clear is that this is the only way.)

I find myself going cold, but I know you will understand, my dearest. I shall do as Martin wished, but only because I must. Martin shall never learn the true reason. He will live the rest of his days thinking himself the most ingenious of men; he will have committed the perfect crime! His wife will be dead, as he planned, but he would not have murdered her.

Now it is time. You are not a religious man I know, but please, my love, pray for me.

Flora'

Jock folded the sheets, replaced them in the envelope and stared vacantly out to sea. Waves broke with monotonous regularity on the beach, but in his imagination he saw a small, frightened figure standing in darkness on the deck of a ship. His lips trembled.

He knew full well the effect these pages would have in the courtroom — these words that could liberate a condemned man — yet Jock hesitated. Once he had told Flora that he was the master of his fate. Now a terrible power lay in his hands and he was exalted yet afraid.

The sound of distant voices coming closer brought him to his feet. He looked across to see the boys returning with their mother.

"I'm hungry!" one called. "Let's eat!" Then he heard his wife's voice — "No! Not until you've washed off all that sand!"

As they splashed in the icy sea Jock's eyes rested on the figure of his wife standing on the edge of the breakers. He looked tenderly at her and knew at last what it was that he had to do.

The lads had built a fire between rocks in a sheltered nook and then they had run off to play while the stout wood burned fiercely. Now it glowed at just the right temperature for cooking the lamb chops and *boerewors* they had brought with them. Jock strode quickly over to it.

He did not hesitate. With but a cursory glance at the papers in his hand he held them to the embers. There was a quick explosive glare. The pages curled and twisted, as if in anguish, then died to grey ashes that stirred in the wind and were gone.

Jock's eyes filled with sudden tears and an icy chill ran through him, then slowly he turned his face to the warmth of the sun.

THE END

Other titles in the Ulverscroft Large Print Series:

TO FIGHT THE WILD
Rod Ansell and Rachel Percy

Lost in uncharted Australian bush, Rod Ansell survived by hunting and trapping wild animals, improvising shelter and using all the bushman's skills he knew.

COROMANDEL
Pat Barr

India in the 1830s is a hot, uncomfortable place, where the East India Company still rules. Amelia and her new husband find themselves caught up in the animosities which seethe between the old order and the new.

THE SMALL PARTY
Lillian Beckwith

A frightening journey to safety begins for Ruth and her small party as their island is caught up in the dangers of armed insurrection.

THE WILDERNESS WALK
Sheila Bishop

Stifling unpleasant memories of a misbegotten romance in Cleave with Lord Francis Aubrey, Lavinia goes on holiday there with her sister. The two women are thrust into a romantic intrigue involving none other than Lord Francis.

THE RELUCTANT GUEST
Rosalind Brett

Ann Calvert went to spend a month on a South African farm with Theo Borland and his sister. They both proved to be different from her first idea of them, and there was Storr Peterson — the most disturbing man she had ever met.

ONE ENCHANTED SUMMER
Anne Tedlock Brooks

A tale of mystery and romance and a girl who found both during one enchanted summer.

CLOUD OVER MALVERTON
Nancy Buckingham

Dulcie soon realises that something is seriously wrong at Malverton, and when violence strikes she is horrified to find herself under suspicion of murder.

AFTER THOUGHTS
Max Bygraves

The Cockney entertainer tells stories of his East End childhood, of his RAF days, and his post-war showbusiness successes and friendships with fellow comedians.

MOONLIGHT AND MARCH ROSES
D. Y. Cameron

Lynn's search to trace a missing girl takes her to Spain, where she meets Clive Hendon. While untangling the situation, she untangles her emotions and decides on her own future.

NURSE ALICE IN LOVE
Theresa Charles

Accepting the post of nurse to little Fernie Sherrod, Alice Everton could not guess at the romance, suspense and danger which lay ahead at the Sherrod's isolated estate.

POIROT INVESTIGATES
Agatha Christie

Two things bind these eleven stories together — the brilliance and uncanny skill of the diminutive Belgian detective, and the stupidity of his Watson-like partner, Captain Hastings.

LET LOOSE THE TIGERS
Josephine Cox

Queenie promised to find the long-lost son of the frail, elderly murderess, Hannah Jason. But her enquiries threatened to unlock the cage where crucial secrets had long been held captive.

THE TWILIGHT MAN
Frank Gruber

Jim Rand lives alone in the California desert awaiting death. Into his hermit existence comes a teenage girl who blows both his past and his brief future wide open.

DOG IN THE DARK
Gerald Hammond

Jim Cunningham breeds and trains gun dogs, and his antagonism towards the devotees of show spaniels earns him many enemies. So when one of them is found murdered, the police are on his doorstep within hours.

THE RED KNIGHT
Geoffrey Moxon

When he finds himself a pawn on the chessboard of international espionage with his family in constant danger, Guy Trent becomes embroiled in moves and countermoves which may mean life or death for Western scientists.

TIGER TIGER
Frank Ryan

A young man involved in drugs is found murdered. This is the first event which will draw Detective Inspector Sandy Woodings into a whirlpool of murder and deceit.

CAROLINE MINUSCULE
Andrew Taylor

Caroline Minuscule, a medieval script, is the first clue to the whereabouts of a cache of diamonds. The search becomes a deadly kind of fairy story in which several murders have an other-worldly quality.

LONG CHAIN OF DEATH
Sarah Wolf

During the Second World War four American teenagers from the same town join the Army together. Forty-two years later, the son of one of the soldiers realises that someone is systematically wiping out the families of the four men.

THE LISTERDALE MYSTERY
Agatha Christie

Twelve short stories ranging from the light-hearted to the macabre, diverse mysteries ingeniously and plausibly contrived and convincingly unravelled.

TO BE LOVED
Lynne Collins

Andrew married the woman he had always loved despite the knowledge that Sarah married him for reasons of her own. So much heartache could have been avoided if only he had known how vital it was to be loved.

ACCUSED NURSE
Jane Converse

Paula found herself accused of a crime which could cost her her job, her nurse's reputation, and even the man she loved, unless the truth came to light.

A GREAT DELIVERANCE
Elizabeth George

Into the web of old houses and secrets of Keldale Valley comes Scotland Yard Inspector Thomas Lynley and his assistant to solve a particularly savage murder.

'E' IS FOR EVIDENCE
Sue Grafton

Kinsey Millhone was bogged down on a warehouse fire claim. It came as something of a shock when she was accused of being on the take. She'd been set up. Now she had a new client — herself.

A FAMILY OUTING IN AFRICA
Charles Hampton and Janie Hampton

A tale of a young family's journey through Central Africa by bus, train, river boat, lorry, wooden bicycle and foot.

THE PLEASURES OF AGE
Robert Morley

The author, British stage and screen star, now eighty, is enjoying the pleasures of age. He has drawn on his experiences to write this witty, entertaining and informative book.

THE VINEGAR SEED
Maureen Peters

The first book in a trilogy which follows the exploits of two sisters who leave Ireland in 1861 to seek their fortune in England.

A VERY PAROCHIAL MURDER
John Wainwright

A mugging in the genteel seaside town turned to murder when the victim died. Then the body of a young tearaway is washed ashore and Detective Inspector Lyle is determined that a second killing will not go unpunished.

DEATH ON A HOT SUMMER NIGHT
Anne Infante

Micky Douglas is either accident-prone or someone is trying to kill him. He finds himself caught in a desperate race to save his ex-wife and others from a ruthless gang.

HOLD DOWN A SHADOW
Geoffrey Jenkins

Maluti Rider, with the help of four of the world's most wanted men, is determined to destroy the Katse Dam and release a killer flood.

THAT NICE MISS SMITH
Nigel Morland

A reconstruction and reassessment of the trial in 1857 of Madeleine Smith, who was acquitted by a verdict of Not Proven of poisoning her lover, Emile L'Angelier.

SEASONS OF MY LIFE
Hannah Hauxwell and Barry Cockcroft

The story of Hannah Hauxwell's struggle to survive on a desolate farm in the Yorkshire Dales with little money, no electricity and no running water.

TAKING OVER
Shirley Lowe and Angela Ince

A witty insight into what happens when women take over in the boardroom and their husbands take over chores, children and chickenpox.

AFTER MIDNIGHT STORIES,
The Fourth Book Of

A collection of sixteen of the best of today's ghost stories, all different in style and approach but all combining to give the reader that special midnight shiver.

DEATH TRAIN
Robert Byrne

The tale of a freight train out of control and leaking a paralytic nerve gas that turns America's West into a scene of chemical catastrophe in which whole towns are rendered helpless.

THE ADVENTURE OF THE CHRISTMAS PUDDING
Agatha Christie

In the introduction to this short story collection the author wrote "This book of Christmas fare may be described as 'The Chef's Selection'. I am the Chef!"

RETURN TO BALANDRA
Grace Driver

Returning to her Caribbean island home, Suzanne looks forward to being with her parents again, but most of all she longs to see Wim van Branden, a coffee planter she has known all her life.

SKINWALKERS
Tony Hillerman

The peace of the land between the sacred mountains is shattered by three murders. Is a 'skinwalker', one who has rejected the harmony of the Navajo way, the murderer?

A PARTICULAR PLACE
Mary Hocking

How is Michael Hoath, newly arrived vicar of St. Hilary's, to meet the demands of his flock and his strained marriage? Further complications follow when he falls hopelessly in love with a married parishioner.

A MATTER OF MISCHIEF
Evelyn Hood

A saga of the weaving folk in 18th century Scotland. Physician Gavin Knox was desperately seeking a cure for the pox that ravaged the slums of Glasgow and Paisley, but his adored wife, Margaret, stood in the way.